Love and the Muses and all the luscious things

Love and the Muses and all the luscious things

by Kyle Gougeon

ISBN:9798343801385

Cover Art Credit to Tammy Gougeon

Other works by Kyle Gougeon:
Love and Cupid and all the sultry things

And an additional 24 unpublished novels, visit the
author's page on Facebook for information.

For Tammy, my forever Muse. I am a few words closer to telling you.

This book is dedicated to Mom.

Preface

In acknowledgement of the elements shaping and misshaping this human existence, to those mentioned in this story and in honor of those yet unnamed:

AMBITION and his chessboard
AWARENESS and his clenching teeth
CERTAINTY snacks and naps like a child
CONTENTMENT speaks very little and lays in the grass
DOUBT and the brutal way it carries you
ENVY and his cold hungry eyes
FATE and his paths and his hands
FEAR in its jungle
FEVER and her heart as tender as that of a bent angel
GENEROSITY is shy but we know his name
HAPPINESS is too young and light for such weapons
HOPE and the hearts she seeks
KISSES throughout and throughout and throughout
LEGS and how they carry and dance and dream
LOVECANDY and her burglar's eyes
MORNING and all she brings and all she hides
NIGHT is the creator and keeper of secrets
NIGHTMOVES and oh how he sings
OLD HANDS with eyes of betrayal
PAST is skinny and shows us his ribs

PEACE and her grand entrances
PLEASURE is not afraid of the daylight
POISON PEN leaves love notes for my wife and drinks
SADNESS and its thumbs and hands
SATISFACTION sits so heavily
SPARKS come invited like an old friend and drinks wine
STICKY senses our passion and takes a swim
STRENGTH and its hounds and its gardens
SURRENDER is so pale and gray
TIME doesn't understand how to move in straight lines
WORRY collects his treasures in dumpsters
WORK with his massive boulders and burdens

Each have their moments whether brief or unbearable, I hope you enjoy the tale to come.

The Narrator
September 2024

My Love keeps the Muses warm in her flowerpots until they grow strong and aware enough, independent enough to take shelter beneath the rosebushes. It is there they will be safe until they are called. If I am to believe what I have been told, each muse becomes without knowing their name or time or destination. Love has had no hand in their creation. She comforts them, she sings to them and smiles at them, she protects and encourages them.

Love is an older muse, she is carried by a 500 year soul. She was mothered once, and now she mothers. She does not direct or scold them, their freedom is natural and given and absolute, she speaks lovingly and patiently to them. There is a unique safety here, the muses cling to our roses, they hide within them as if in a forest. The sunlight teases them through the blooms and the thorns, and when the muses venture into the grass the rain nips at their heels and chases them like squealing delighted children. I can not see them, but I trust they are there. Love can hear them, she is always aware, I see her smile when she tells me they are playing in her long hair.

Neither of us remember when they first arrived, that day arrived and left unannounced. They find our modest home to be a sanctuary. Now that their river has long been dry. We are a step from the paradise, we are a haven from the loss and the search. Our humble home of passion, it has a quiet longing beauty, perhaps more noticed in passing than sought. It is all we wish for.

There should always be a space for Love and the muses in this world, even if it should just be here, in this peaceful corner. Our yard is stoic and sometimes stubborn and speaks in tongues I am beginning to understand. I do not always, but I have today. It hasn't complained as we planted lines and clusters of colors today. It has laid still and flat and mostly lazy. Maybe it believes it is getting dressed for the ball. But the soil gets into our skin, it gets into our souls.

I dig one last hole and catch my Love's eye and hers catch mine. We live within a slow pause, within a hesitation of the mystery. We live in the hum of a quiet constant simmering Fever. The Fever is alive and old and more fierce than the tides. It is a refuge, a rest, it is volatile as it comforts, it soothes us as if we were volcanoes, it rubs our private stomachs and legs, it brings our hands to our faces. We can't embrace the last and the tired, we embrace the new and the next and keep it all safe in our little sanctuary nestled off the maps, somewhere between the ocean and the mountains.

She has my lover's smile and my lover's voice, and I am home here. We can rise to unfathomable heights, unrestrained highs, and parachute down, hand in hand, somewhere close to earth, somewhere close to now, somewhere within the peace which rests between want and need. Somewhere within the comfortable arms of knowing.

And the muses have found a trust here, they have found a home here. They stay and they are welcome for as long as they desire to be here. They chase away the insects and the noise, they chase away the worry and the hurry. I know this by the way Love hums and whispers and waters the plants.

There must always be a force, there must be words pushed into the needs of this world, there must be a place in this world. For all of this. I carry love in pails and baskets, in buckets and in my pockets. There are long tireless days,

days that have no aggression, days that have simple passion, days we do not chase and they do not chase us. There is light where darkness can not be, there is calm where nothing more needs to be done. There are moments that can not be stolen or borrowed or even owned.

This is the first chapter of a story that is happy to admit it is but a living, breathing dream. The story of Love and Leo, just a beg and a distance from the universe and its hands. We are but a moment within a drop, captured from a drip. I am yours and you are mine, for what feels to us like eternity.

I know this world can not be perfect, it can not find rest, but it can not be itself or contain itself without Love and the Muses and all the lucious things.

I am in a chair, I pull my legs beneath me, they are heavy with contentment and heavier with ease. I am loveenraptured, I am lovecooled. It is time to find steps again, it is time to find movement. The clouds are coming, they are racing themselves, the sky's stomach is churning and rolling over on itself. A storm is coming and bringing an end to this afternoon, a thunderstorm is dipping and dripping its heavy brow and everyone and everything is seeking cover. And just waiting.

I stand at the back door as though I am standing guard. The lightning has begun to lick its crackling lips. Love is inside, shuffling the dishes. I shift from leg to leg, as if shifting from past to present. Present to future. I am at peace and at odds, in this moment. I can see for as far as my eyes allow. My heart sees much farther, it drinks and absorbs, swallows and understands. The lightning has bowed to the winds, and now the rains have started. They are trying to blur the lines between the mud and the dirt. But as always, the ferocity is brief and under spoken, the loud is gone and there are no pieces to pick up. The bravery was lost within the bravado.

There is a little wetness to the ground, the sky hangs its belly low, gray and green. It just needed to yell and scream a bit, it needed a stretch. We are fine within our little promise. I muddle about the grass and wander to the rosebushes. I want them to know this is a harbor, this is a calm and a canvas. The muses venture into the yard again.

They are free here. They are free to roam, free to remain, free to leave. They drink from the roses and eat honey from the lips of the bees. They are safe and rarely look into our windows. If there were ever a proper place for the muses to be, somewhere between now and then, somewhere between ours and theirs, between heaven and earth. It is here.

There is not a fire that burns slower and longer than happily ever after. The heavy simplicity sits, the newness cascades. Forever has its legs up, its ankles are around our necks and its toes are in our hair. It is trying to press us into a wild kiss it promises will last just a moment but we know it will last an hour. I have a hand that won't let go and you have a hand in mine that aches just the same. Our hands are reaching for 500 years lost and holding onto today before it becomes yesterday. I will find you in the morning, I will find your eyes. I will tell you about all the things I thought about after the world ran itself still and silent.

BEING

Our hands are creators. Our smiles are dancers. Our dreams are lovers. I am learning to see with your patience and optimism. Somebody's weight has dropped from my shoulders. I can feel your bravery and your confidence. I am slowly absorbing it, one spoonful of sugar at a time. I am evolving, there is nothing to take, nothing to waste, nothing to steal, nothing to hide, nothing to keep, but everything to share.

It is our penance and our promise and our adoration, our love plays in the breezes, it rises to the sky, it hides in the grass. And it returns to our lips and fingertips. We will be just fine, you and I, between the hard lines of the fences, beyond the shadows of the days, in the whispers shared across pillows, in the whispers that dare the dark. There are truths born and shared between hearts and mouths and arms and hips and legs. There are truths that can not be unfelt and unheard. There are truths found in the midnight eyes and within the pressings and the lashings. There are truths waiting every morning and carrying you through the day.

We can press so tightly together, heart to heart, there is no room for light upon our backs. We can roll our love between our kisses and knees and wishes. Let all the sand stay in its place, let the clouds burst from their cages. Give me your hands and the sounds of our wedding bells.

Today is alive and pumping and pulsing loveblood, and the soup and the spoils lay just outside in the heat. We can keep our moments and our minutes to ourselves. We are fire, and we are alive, right here. There is no searching or lurking disaster, we are free, we are us. When trust and pleasure take you by your arms, when everything else crumbles and you are left to know only what you know, the rest is inviting, it is a burn.

Just being is such a small breath within the magic. It is the stark and naked easy part. And then there are the layers, the calling layers, those that seem so frail and fragile. They are all you can't forget, all you can't surrender. The suffering of the subtle things which rest just below the lucious things. Suddenly you can not tell the difference between the soulful things and the everyday things, you walk and talk the way you are supposed to, you smile the way you are supposed to smile, and you hold onto everything that was meant to be in your loveheated hands. The way it was intended.

These are the syrupy, dripping hours some have forgotten and some have never known. There is pleasure in their fatigue, fatigue in their quiet, laziness in their minutes. It has been years, now. Our modest little house pulled in its legs and planted them like roots. It showed us and we followed its example. There will be no wandering now. There is a softness about our sanctuary, we are rarely a whisper beyond its edges. There are no ghosts in the attic, no scars on our lips or eyes. Everything was before yesterday and can not touch us now.

These are the days I see what I must do, when I look through the window I can only envision myself with Love. These are some of the many days we have what we want. I have left my boots outside the front door, stuffed my socks and worries inside them. I won't need them the rest of the day, I won't need them until after tomorrow. The work is finished for now, the lovelabors gently elbow their way in. I smell the cut grass, there is a hole calling to be dug, there are flowers calling for water. These are the breezes, this is the shade. The sun comes to my back from high above. These are the truths, this is the reward.

The weatherman called for it to be hot and sultry this afternoon, I am still deciding if I trust him with my picnic. I am within my new learned element, I am in my new light, my new life. Love is around the corner, she is humming, her hands are in the soil. I believe the earth needs to be upon us, she needs our fingers as we need her. I haven't had a tail behind me for some time, some years, not with Love. I haven't had one to drag or one to tuck and run, not with Love. We spread our promises like sculptures all around. Promises to evolve and thrive, promises to quiet and slow ourselves and enjoy. To live and adore, to explore and expand, to huddle and hold, to answer and embrace and respect and kiss. To acknowledge the wants and not be haunted by them, to acknowledge the haves and bring them into our crowded bed.

My feet face forward with confidence to dance. This is a pleasant ending to an afternoon. I hear a wilderness call, I hear a wildness call. I sense loveambition lurking. But first, the meandering silent chores, but first the unassuming, but first the joy. Ours is a lovejournery, a simmering forever, we relish every step without counting them. It is lovemath. Moments pass without markings, days pass with no names, it is our lovely eternity. We prefer it in a wash, in a bath.

The simplest, most sensual state of existence is being. It is the most difficult to achieve. There are no maps, no landmarks, no instructions. It can not be sought or found. The state of being can not be taught or studied or learned. You can try the taste of the coals or the flames that live in the fire, you will be burned all the same, as you are. You can flip or leap, roll in it, deny it or defy it. You have to know her name, and you have to believe in it, as sure as you are walking and breathing, souldressed and talking. I know her name. It is Love. And I am happily in her fire. I had longed for it, now I am scorched every day. The passion can be dressed with milk, it can be hidden in gravy. Passion without hesitation or guess or thought. Passion which cascades with all the luscious things.

We don't beg for the end of the day, we beg no forgiveness. We seek torturously slow, thick simplicity. When Love is not queen in the yard, she is an absolute lady, with all the beauty and depths a woman can offer. When I am not king in the yard, I am a renaissance man. We happily toil until evening breaks through the sky and reminds us our stomachs are hungry. We have secrets we keep as our own, dreams we lay out beneath the moon, we walk holding dirty hands.

There are candle farms beyond the trees, the sun is sleeping somewhere beyond our sight and even our memory. Our house is napping behind us. We will create our own light tonight. Our poor town has been ravaged by a summer's day, I can hear it gasping in the distance. I turn off the outside lights to remind it, there is still a quiet corner here.

Love's sleepy eyes appear beside me. There is a gentle darkness about that follows us inside. The day is over, and Night is too impatient for hesitation. The clocks have stopped and only our hands are moving in a delicious twist, with a tingle within a moment within a sense draped in a wet promise. The shadows tip their hats and cover their ears, the blankets pretend not to notice. Because lovers need their moments, north and south and to and fro, boiled and unbothered, lost, cast, the wild hairs and the sighs, and all the luscious things these walls and windows and doors hope to contain.

I ask, 'Love are you sleeping yet?'. I want her to lay her head upon her pillow so close to mine, I need her breath because this is the most exquisite night we have ever known. I want her to find her peace and her strength, place her cheek to mine, trust her cheek against mine. I want her burdens upon my shoulders, I will carry them tomorrow. Because this is our night, and the darkness and silence outside know it.

'What you do to my soul, giving it these arms and legs,' I say. Love kisses me to tell me she is not sleeping yet. I can see her eyes beyond her hair, I can nearly reach them. This is when the feet and the steps fall into calm, this is how we like to travel, within these private moments, warm and inexplicable and unsharable moments, comfortably lost between night and day. These hours rise and fall as they wish, these hours caught between contentment and bliss. They belong to innocents and lovers, and no one else.

The Night's chalkboard was still spread wide across her sky when I came inside. I had nothing to write on it, I had nothing to splash on it. There will be nothing for Her to clean tomorrow. Love and I took to the quiet of our sanctuary, without dares or challenges, with only promises.   I   can tell by her breathing, Love is listening to my last touches, soft and drifting upon her shoulders, her arms, fleeting across her hip. My head is so heavy upon my pillow. This day has finally given up the last of its trumpets. I haven't heard a noise for some time, not from within our house, not from outside. I might be the last standing, the last to surrender. Love's voice curls around my side and swirls past my brow. 'Goodnight, my Leo, I love you.' And then her words vanish without a crackle, without the slightest smoke. Ease settles around me and upon me, I find one touch, a single finger holds it upon the back of her hand. Yes, this is another glorious night.

I can fall into the calm and taste no other sensation. I can fall into sleep lovesatisfied and lovestormed. Beyond the sheets and the covers that bury this sanctuary into safety there are no regrets and no unpaid wishes. Just peace and dreams until sleep transforms into beautiful colors.

The exact hour is lost to me and I do not search it out. I lay in this moment a little longer, asking forgiveness from the next. Consciousness and I are playing a cat and mouse game. Love's face is beside me in our room, and there is no where I would rather be. Had I known how fat and thick and rich life would become once it stepped aside, once it became evolution and endearment and simplicity, I might have tried it earlier. The chains fell so easily, like a gift.

Love sleeps like one who is held and not captured, her contentment is spreading. In one moment she breathes like a mystic, in the next like a mystery, she is safe and protected and adored beyond all of our years. My arms and legs convince my mind to follow. I lay beside the answer to so many questions. I kiss her one more time. I lay in her honest embrace, because the truths have too many faces and too many motives. I want one more kiss for understanding, one for patience, one more kiss for passion, and one for perseverance, one kiss for desire and ambition, and one more upon her forehead. One more kiss for dreams and bliss, one soft upon her lips and one into the universe. One kiss for living as we do, one kiss to forget the past, one for all the tomorrows, the tomorrows as they come, insecure or proud, small or tall, wet or mild, they are ours and ours and ours.

There is never a new slick moment lost, not when we are simply being us.

19

The coffee is proud of itself today, I can smell it through the closed door. It has come to an agreement with the two cups and spoon I left out last night, I hear the last pops and gurgles, perhaps it has finished reading the note I leave every night for Love. I am awake and moving about first. All the quieter moments are sprinkled in the air. Today has a lighter purpose, a joyful purpose. It can wait until after breakfast. I will first have coffee with Love. We feel the comfortable hold of luxury, the calm of luxury. The luxury of two working people staying home for one day.

There is a large clock on the wall outside, it is trying not to be ignored, it is trying to hurry the day. It is midmorning, it whispers, it is getting later, it whispers. I tell myself it must be talking to the fences. Love joins me now and we've filled our two chairs. We are waking slowly and lovesmoldering. The direction and the destination of this day are swirling, they have no real weight. Love and I may be the only ones who understand what we will have accomplished by the end of the afternoon. The coffee is working into my eyes. Love sits in a loose robe. This is life without anxiety, this is a dream of being, this is beautiful.

There will be lovework and lovesweat today, in the pots and in the grass, in the air and the playgrounds of the muses. There will be shovels and shears and water hoses, they speak freedom to our hands, they speak pleasure to our hands. There will be conversations and long comfortable silences, casual strolls and dreaming. The grounds around our modest home will be wet with it. It is for all to see and us to feel.

This one day, for us. But first coffee, first peace. Love touches my hand. 'Where is your mind, Leo?' she says. It is here, around us, above us. A long hair has found my cup and reaches down to my elbow. She smiles and it is 1000 times worse than when she smiled as my bride, the hair hangs, we sit a little longer, and it just gets worse.

She and I share the loveyears with but a word, a glance, this life and this world can count the loveyears, all the way up to five. Forever and always is beyond the reach of the learned numbers. Forever and always have sugar and depth and fire. I kiss her and plead for lovechains, she kisses me and puts them on like wings.

I refill our cups, I look at the magic outside the window. Today is for lovedefiance, it will be gentle. We will ignore all the calls, all the requests, all the demands. We will have dirt and laughter, relaxation, a swim and a steak, and all the hours as they were meant to be. Even the dishes in the sink, the floors, the unmade bed, the laundry, they all seem to urge me back outside. I want to tell her with new words with a lovetongue. I try to do so every day.

We are beginning to break into moving pieces now, I am stretching my legs and she is humming and soaking everything within reach. I am feeling light and casual. I can see Work is beyond the tree line, beyond the boundary and the footbridge. He is beyond where I intend to be today. He is moving his massive boulders and makes no sound of effort, his wide shoulders show no sign of strain. I will be with him tomorrow, he does not speak to me today. His powerful arms and enormous hands shove the boulders like burdens. I nod to him, he has an earnest, trustworthy look. There is a hint of a glimpse of a whisper in his eyes. A memory in his eyes.

The last of the nightshadows have moved aside, there are pools of cool shade here and there, should we need them. There will be color today, we will stretch our yard with color, scratch and work it with color. Love and I smile to each other, our universe is wrapping around us like a nest. Today is bountiful, there is enough for everyone and everything. No one must wait, no one must be impatient, no one must be greedy. We are being lovegorged. There may have been stains behind us, stains beneath us, stains from where we have been and what we have known. They fade further with each step. We leave them to yesterday, yesterday can keep them like treasures, we have our own.

The day has been fueled, it has been ignited. It is afternoon, I am kneeling in the grass, there is a pleasant sweat on my arms. I hear Love murmuring around the corner in the higher pitch of a grandmother. I have dug my last hole, I seek her out for a kiss. 'Can you see the Muses?' she says. I can not. But I do not doubt they are here. Something is wrinkling the roses, something is thorning the stems. Perhaps they are uncertain of me and hiding. I already have my muse.

I believe it is time to admire and rest. Of the countless things Love has taught me, one is generally clear and loud.

If you listen, the universe is telling you. There were no timelines or deadlines or quotas today. The years and the miles are speaking to my joints. We have labored just to the crumbling edges of pleasure's reach. Beyond that is not a place we wish to be.

I look around and over and through and into our fantastic grounds. My eyes go all the way to the trees. I see Work, with his shoulders and his pride. He is washing his hands now. He is humble, solid and impressive. I walk over to him, to shake his hand. His penetrating eyes do not name me or rename me. He knows I have always done all I can do. It is the honesty, the effort, the perseverance, they are like plates on his table, it is what he eats, and he eats well. I feel I know him and admire him, and perhaps he feels the same. Perhaps not an old friend, but a companion, a teacher. Work is always welcome here, I offer him a chair, I offer him an invitation. He politely declines. He always has his own place in this world, it is just not here today.

There are some lingering hours to this day that haven't been spent or used or even noticed. I am thinking they are near our pool. They are the undedicated hours each day quietly possesses but does not admit to, the hours that aren't sorted or predetermined. They are the crazy hours, the ones with legs, the ones that flee. They flesh out the days and weeks and months we all live. They are the nameless hours, the uncounted hours, the ones that don't belong and don't stand in line. They are the hours we cherish. Their reach is longer and bolder than the rest. Me, Love, and them, we all laugh, they were pretty clever choosing their hiding spots this time, pretending they had slipped away.

We dress for the cool waters of the pool and climb in, leg by leg, inch by inch. The satisfaction of this quiet day can not be described. This is the reward beyond the colors and the peace. We sink, we drift, escaping the glorious heat. My elbow bumps into Time herself, and now I know I am right. She floats, passive and relaxed, in the pool out on the patio behind our house. Her eyes are closed, the hands of the clock are nowhere to be found. She floats, unstirring.

Love and I and Time share such moments. She must have chosen to share our afternoon. We do not question or answer. We give her room, we give her space. She will rise and conquer when she chooses to do so. As for me, I let my arms and legs float. Love comes to me for a kiss, and another, and we kiss again as though it is new.

Contentment and Certainty have been running through our yard like wild children all day. I raise my head to look for them. They are over in the corner, they are in the shade, they are in the hush, they are having snacks and about to take a nap in the bushes. We are all exactly where we need to be.

There is a name for every day, there is a number for every hour within. There is a sleepy hot satisfaction just within, a syrup, a truth, in the cringing moments. There is a place we can go, Love and I, it exists after the words have failed, after the words have missed, after the movements have stopped. We don't seek it, we aren't called to it. There is a warmth as fragile as light. We can't find it with our hands, we can't wrap it in our arms. But it knows our dreams. We know it, during our perfect days, during the surprising days, the private days. The days we go nowhere else, when all we need is here. I hope there are more safe homes in the world for such a place.

It is easy to surrender to passion, today, it is easy to surrender to devotion. Our eyes know why our hearts ache. Our eyes speak their own language so our mouths won't listen. Sometimes there are only two people in the world. Time climbs out of the pool, we look the other way as she dresses. She puts the hands back on the clock and puts her hands back onto the throat of the world. There is going to be a record now, by her will it is four o'clock. It is going to be documented now. We are part of a growing history now. The slow and the tranquil and the easy are going to have to show their faces.

I want to be here just a little longer, at least until the heat dries the splashes Time made, until the water burns from the patio. Until my hands are filled, until my heart is overflowing. I want to stay here for as long as my mouth is raw with kisses. Love sets her blue eyes upon me, they steam across the water. I want to stay until I have forgotten all I have known and learned. It is just Love and I and all our pieces. Let's pretend we have not already been healed, let's dance like you don't know my shoulders yet. If it all becomes too thick, let it be a rope to climb up or climb down.

These are the moments, just being, with their heaviness and simplicity. These are the moments that wash my face clean. These are the moments I hold in my hands and rub through my hair. These are the moments that make my soul rage, they pound in my chest. The light does not hide from the dark, it isn't afraid anymore. We are simply sitting in chairs, and her hand touches mine. They are the moments I want to find the words to describe.

Time and Contentment and Certainty have all left, and it is just Love and I, it is just us, as we were meant to be. 'What is for dinner tonight?' she asks. And as I promised it will be steak and gravy and passion and bread. The wind is blowing, we are turning lights on inside the house. The Elements are rattling their cages, and I smile, because I know they are not confined. The rain has started and tells us to stay inside. We are exactly where and how we are supposed to be, with my lines and her curves, her sweet smile and my raw.

Oh this hush, this wonderful luscious blanket of being, where she runs to me and I to her. Being is better than been, being nurses us through the landscapes and the hardships. Being drowns out what we feel we must do and what we need to do. And being with Love requires nothing else.

I watch a humming rain find its way through the leaves and branches, I stand at an opened door facing away from the world, a door leading to ours. Our yard and our labors won't get sick from it, the summer sky will appear again before night. I feel as though I can see the difference between the natural and the real and all we have been shown. The rain steams in the green and the lush, it steams in our privacy. There is nothing more to do today than eat and enjoy the waves of the lovesilk.

I can see now all the pretty things, they drape everything in a comfortable silence. Delicious smells come to me when Love opens the door. She has been dressing the empty plates. It will be just a bit longer, which is fine, because these new hours following the rain have lost their panic and hurry. Our appetites come from what we have already devoured, the heat and the truths between afternoon and evening, and the comfort between evening and finding our way to our bed. This night can walk the way it wishes.

'Did you hear the Muses playing just then?' Love asks. And I did not. One day their sounds may come to me. I believe in the innocence and the beauty of the muses. But for now the bugs are dancing and the birds are on the hunt, there is a cat on the prowl and the dogs are howling in the distance. Wet or not, the world rolls on without asking permission. At the stretch of our yard, beyond the small white fence, beyond the unsteady gate, a movement catches my eye. I take a step into the dying rain to see what it is. It is not the mystery, it is not the muses, it is not Time coming for a second visit.

The Past is out there, looking towards us with its sickly sunken eyes. He is somber and hoping to change our lovecharged mood. He lifts his ragged gray shirt and shows me his ribs. Love is in the light and the glare from the kitchen window keeps her from seeing what I see. I offer him a silent stare, the Past can look but he can not stay. There is no room at the table, there is no room in the house. He can use yesterday's newspaper to keep his head dry. He draws neither my sympathy or curiosity. 'You can take your things with you' I whisper. The Past begins to pull his chains through the grass and makes it mud and silently exits and disappears.

Love and I are here and in the calm and in the fire and we speak certain words and live in certain ways. I seem to have visions and memories of only these last five years. The old centuries have aged and crawled, the new centuries are eager to come, eager to stay, eager to be kept. And I am patient to have them. The old centuries are dragged in Past's chains, they are thick in his memories. I haven't a cup or umbrella to offer. I haven't a kindness or insult to hurl. The Past is a shell of himself, he has lost his voice and lost his weight. He shuffles and labors along, down a lonely road seeking other houses.

The empty plates are now crushed and piled, they are overflowing. Love has pulled her hair back down. Love has called to me with her steps. She can feed my strength, put some air into it with a look and a gasp. There are still some loveshouts and lovehours left untouched and unspent. Tomorrow heaves itself onto the table, but ends up falling to the floor, looking for scraps. My thirst is wet, and my hunger is loud. My heart is full and my soul is talking. Everything is just how it should be, everything is in its true and raw condition. I hold Love by her hands, I hold Love by her eyes, I hold Love with the kiss I was supposed to give her 400

28

years ago, I sneak another across her cheek, the one we missed 150 years ago.

I kiss her and she offers one in return for today, and another for tomorrow. We know the simplicity and luxury of being.

LEAPING

I barely have time to say anything in my deep hushed bedtime voice, my words just managed to reach Love and her breaths. The Nightmoves are here, heavier than whitenoise. Love has opened her arms and smiles, my legs haven't yet unstraightened to do their dances, my arms have not leapt from their shoulders. My hands, I will just leave them where they are, or use them to silence myself. Nightmoves once again has accepted his open invitation, and oh how he sings, he draws us in close long before the allure of the chorus. He is wearing those shoes, those fine fine shoes, and is easing into his steps, his steps are sliding side to side. His words are showering us before we can relax, they are taking possession before we can find the lights.

Nightmoves voice is slick and rich with soul and want. His lyrics pull our skin, his tone goes deep as a tribal drum and then higher than the voice of an angel. He speaks of desires that twist the comforter in luscious snaking piles.

The windows are covered, the bed is drowning, we reach to block the clocks and the ears and all the rest of the eyes. The sheets are stolen, all our senses are stolen, any fatigue has been thrown to the floor. Nightmoves says dreams need some sugar if they are going to bake all night. He provokes us slowly and prods us gently, there is no escaping. He sings, he does a little tilt and a shimmy, his hand is hiding his eyes, our hands are hiding our eyes.

We let the worlds bleed and blend once again. Those which do no harm with enthusiasm, those which belong with enthusiasm, those which answer questions, those which have what we need. Nightmoves and his alluring style and pleasure dances, his sultry soothing voice, the distance between his steps and us is rapidly vanishing. And ooh, his songs, and oh, his talents, he quietly blends the light with the darkness. He ushered himself into our room in a loveshuffle, he pencils his favorite words on the walls. I dare to peek between my fingers to see his face. His lovegrimaces suggest he might exit and his songs will linger for a while.

Love and I ask for no pushes and we receive no pushes, we know the heat has no boundaries. We understand the lovefalls and the loveclimbs. The dance has no deception, it has no beginning or end. The last of Nightmoves voice is a low hum in the room, oh so low, he leaves with his hat, his steps are pronounced all the way to the door. His eyes were the last, and they have flown off like bats, and now we are alone, together again. The aftermath is quiet and provocative, personal and inspired. The room feels as though it swells with flowers and candy and stew and simmering. These are the last true moments of this night, the last we will know, the last we will remember.

There are moments the Elements try to leave for us, not create for us, moments of linger and leisure they pretend to have forgotten they left behind. They roll about us, they hover over us, they exist just in the corner of our eyes. They are heavy as stone, they are light and alive. Some die and some fade and some become our memories. Nightmoves comes and goes as he wishes. Our moods are fresh and flesh and flash and eased, and suddenly tired.

Sleep will find no struggle to wash into our bones tonight, our lovelabors have earned it. Sleep is the ugly sister of Night, and she comes like she knows it. My hands are crippled, Love's lips are crippled. The Night is the creator and keeper of some secrets, her steps are gentle as they circle our bed. She is telling her sister to play no tricks tonight. I find Love and hold her, somewhere in the darkness she is pressed to me, she will be held in these arms, my arms, until tomorrow.

Work is out of its cave and in the front yard and bellows at me before the alarm can sound. I can hear him and my eyes open. I know, I know. I ask if I might have two cups of coffee, he knows me, he tells me to have three. I have nowhere to run, I have no need to run. He stands heavy and solid in front of our house. He paces patient circles around my boots. He will have my grit today, he will have my attention today. Work lumbers close to the door, he doesn't call my name, he doesn't ask for my soul. It is morning and now he is calling.

His broad shoulders won't be bullied or bothered, his hard earnest face won't be mocked. Here are my boots, here is my lunch, we can walk side by side or he can ride with me. Work has a presence and a purpose that brings a flood of fond memories. Memories of a man from another time. He has a grip and a hold, an undeniable walk that pushes his undeniable steps. I am ready, finally. I feel we have the same breath, we speak with the same voice.

Work saunters in his way, he comes out of the clouds, he rises from the earth, he steps into the snow and the rain, he leans into the heat and the cold. He doesn't recognize the difficult or the can't. He is dedicated and tireless and true. My boots are on and I am on time and we are speaking of things which must be done and things which have to be done. There is no mention of what we would like to do. Want comes later, want waits like a dog. Want comes after the thirst and after the hunger, Work has stepped into the line and he is holding his place.

The trenches of the butcher's shop are laid open and wide. We come in, one by one, behinds its doors, beneath its lights, there in the chill we have all agreed to manage. The coolers and freezers work at our hands, they work at our backs, they work at our joints. The knives are restless whenever they lay still, the tables heave and the racks are overflowing and the carts of meat roll endlessly through the door. The man at the cutting block growls, and then laughs, and breaks into a story about a fishing boat, and then a motorcycle. We bare our arms to prove we have never tattooed the name of an angel on our skin. We talk over the noise of what we walk through, the trimmings, the drippings, the meat and the blood.

There are three of us, sometimes four, the men trying to feed a village and all its visitors. It is best not to think about the numbers and how they stand tall before us. The math is difficult, three against thousands. The long odds make us smile, the challenge makes us move. The cold chases us and we never sweat, but that offers no relief from the strain. This is what we have agreed to do, and day after day, we return for a seemingly endless encore. We come to the coolers, we come to the cave, we come to one of Work's playground.

I walk out into the public view, into the waves of the traffic. To gauge our persistence, to observe our condition, we are swimming, we are not winning but we are not losing. The village is hungry today. We are not here to battle, we are here to satisfy. I shake the chill from my fingers. I can look down a long aisle and see a pleasant day hanging like a photograph on the other side of the front doors. It is not for us, we have hours to go.

The villagers and the visitors grumble, they come dressed to shop, they come dressed for the sun and the beach, they come dressed to complain as though it is a pleasure. Their voices run into mud like a foreign language, their faces blur into a line of opened mouths. The floor groans beneath the crowd today, the meat cases ache from the hands today. I push back through the door, the cold is waiting, I show it my arms.

We outlast the hours, we outlast the boxes and endless plastic and the pounds and pounds and pounds. This is our labor, this is our service. We all exit the building, intact and in one piece. We feel that first stunning grasp of the evening's warmth. 'See you tomorrow,' we all say. Those worries and pains stay behind the doors when they close behind us. We can take off those other faces. Now we get to go home to our lives and our lovers. That is what we have earned, that is why our muscles burn for forgiveness. The hours which keep us are abruptly over. We are released to the hours we want and need.

Love has made it home before me, her day is piled neatly to the right, outside the front door, I leave mine on the left. I walk inside and find our always kiss, our there you are kiss, our another kiss, our here again kiss. Her steps are not what I follow, they lead to where I need to be. It is a constant comfort, a repeated kindness, a reminder of a whisper of a dream.

The thickness is real, it surrounds us, it is inside, it is outside. We leave a light on, but not to find our way. We are here. I join Love on the patio, the evening air is removing the ache and the chill from my skin. And after mopping and sweeping the mansions at the beach, she is preparing flowerpots, she is humming, she is making room. 'New muses are coming,' she says.

Perhaps these I will see.

The dust and the stink of the day is falling from us, it falls to our feet and then chases itself away. It is just Love and I and her kindness, it is just Love and I and her gentleness. It is just us, in the sweet, in the light, in the depths we find we can hold in our hands, in the quieter moments that stretch past conversation, the quieter moments that speak of trust.

Night is coming through the trees, she is coming across the lawn, her legs are out of her dress. She comes with her swirling persuasion, but we are not yet ready. We let go of our long day of labor, and it releases us. Love and I are released into our wild, we don't have to remember, and we don't have to be reminded, this is where we belong. Love is giving all that has been potted a shower, I am reaching for another cold drink. The talk of the day is over, and it is not tomorrow we turn to, tomorrow will always be there. We are here, we are fluid and in place, we are Love and Leo. The rest of the world can remain deaf and blind for the moment.

Ambition and Generosity are out in the lawn, enjoying the peace. They sit in the blue iron chairs, there is a chessboard on the blue iron table between them. I can't hear what they are saying, I can't tell who is winning. It seems to be a friendly match, they appear to applaud each other's moves. They dressed casually and sip their drinks through straws. I see them smile and laugh, they come here to relax. We are all free beyond freedom, perhaps helped beyond burden.

I prepare a simple meal for us, something to return some strength to our want and bones. We will dine outside, where the air mingles fresh, it is crawling over me. The air is healing though I am not broken, I am bent, never broken, never bothered, never bewildered or discouraged. Sweat and labor are companions, but never bedmates. There is but one for me and one for her. There are some lovecalls coming from our bed, there are some loverules to be pressed. There are some secret skins to be shown, behind closed doors.

Ambition and Generosity rise from the table and shake hands to part. They will return, their match is not finished, their last moves have not been made or even been considered.

A single long hair rests so heavy upon my shoulder and I leave it, we settle deeper into chairs, enjoying the noisy quiet. The day may rage for some, we have shelter. Our work is done and the chores are resting contentedly until tomorrow. There is but a sip of a drink remaining and the immensity of Night all around us. 'I love you, Leo,' she says, and I leave that upon my hand and lips.

We share the stillness before the lovechaos, we are in the dry before the soak of the loveundress. The light will lose itself and the moments and seconds and hours will have teeth, real and gentle teeth. This is our time to sponge away the last noises of the day. A stiffened simmer has come and the insects are getting restless and the darkness needs to take its place. Love and I are calm, we have no fires to light, no secrets or regrets to burn. Everything becomes a piece and a memory, once all you want is now and here. The luscious and the sultry things drip into a pool.

The payments to be made have been met, there is nothing more to do than just be. There are pillows to be fed, there are touches to be fed. There is a bed that has laid flat and alone all day. The shadows can play, the moon can be juicy. Love stands and adjusts her hips, I stand and my knees betray me for but a moment. She wants one last look at the pots, I join her for one last look, and maybe I will finally see. But this one is a lilly, that one a fairy, this one a snapdragon, that one a dream. Our flowers are sleeping in their soil and the muses are still on their journey. Love stretches and goes inside and I am in agreement.

Today will be wrapped with its name in a calendar, it will hang on a wall until it is stored in a drawer. It will be remembered only for what we said and what we dared. Tomorrow will come first as a bully. Yesterday will chase us like a menace. This is the way unmarked and unnamed days advance and age. Days not signed by birthdays or anniversaries or accomplishments. The days can end hard, they can end with a sickening landing. They can fall into lines, they can form lazy piles, they can stumble clumsily, just to be moved, boxed, organized, and moved again. Or they can be days like these, when Love sighs into the pudding, when Love whispers through the fire, when she stares through the blue in her eyes.

She speaks through the excruciating joyous days. 'I will see you in a few minutes.' She is going to be waiting with a wash of lightning around her, and my bones are going to act their age but only for a minute. There is only room for truth and romance, there is only so much our fingers can hold, the rest our hearts hold in their teeth. 'I will come kiss you in a minute,' I say.

There is one last visitor tonight, I have noticed him at the edges, he teases the shadows and is enjoying the heat. He steps effortlessly through the nets of the night. He makes his way, tiptoeing through the spoils and the droppings. The Poison Pen is gangly, he is nearly all arms and legs, he mirrors my movements, but I don't believe it is to pester me, and I never take it as such. I try to shiver and dance a bit to see if he will, and then raise my hands as though I don't care. He leaps, he shows me the palms of his hands are clean, they have no harm and only passion. I walk towards the light as a way of inviting him closer. He runs like fire through the darkest side of the yard. He will place his feet where I can not always find a place to stand.

The Poison Pen feels like an old friend, he has a look as though he has been through the ages with me. He looks as though he has felt and tasted some of the same mud. I stop moving, to let him catch up, he stops moving, we share a grinning welcome. A man very dear to me named him. Before that he was a presence, but anonymous. He seems pleased to have a name hung on his face. The Poison Pen seems pleased tonight. Pleased with himself, pleased with me. But not obnoxiously so. There are words out there, just within and just beyond my reach. Words for Love. If I can not find them, he will. The Poison Pen follows along like a tall skinny shadow.

He wanders as freely outside as he does in my mind. He skips in and out, he speaks in and out, he discovers in and out. He plays with the words I will shake my head at tomorrow. He chases and then is chased, laughing, laughing, with his peculiar laugh. The Poison Pen plays in the part of my mind I can not find. The place the doctors can not explain and the surgeons can not fix, the machines can not detect it. He releases the juices from the folds and they never find their way to my lips to be spoken, they can race and wrinkle down my arm to only my left hand, I have but to squeeze a pen's ink onto paper. He finds the words I do not know, he finds the words I can not remember. The Poison Pen is an old, old friend I have never spoken to.

I am more his instrument than he is mine. Some words must flow and some must falter, some must be shouted into the world and some whispered into the corner. He has become a vibrant, elusive, and inseparable part of me. He unlocks the unspeakable truths from their cages and forms them into letters and gathers them into syllables and pushes and presses them into words. He rushes to the head of the parade, he slings the words recklessly into free flowing lines, he works without rules or consequences or conscience. The man dear to me is an element, a force himself, and I hope he and the Poison Pen walk together in harmony, arm in arm, when I am not looking.

The Poison Pen can joust, he can fight, he can plead impossible cases, he can speak chaos or in splinters, he knows thick and fluid lovelanguages. He is the one Element which does not seek to influence me, he draws from me, harnesses me more like a sweetness than a danger. I am more of a slow steady bath than a sudden vicious flood.

My eyes are drifting and easing away from themselves. I think my legs are finally considering surrender to this long, long day. I am at peace, at this moment, and I will be at peace in the next. The Poison Pen approaches closer, finally, he walks almost like a bird. He knows I will never fight him, I will never eat him. I will never betray him and he will never betray me. He hugs me almost like a brother does, he has a whimsical knowing smile.

I stagger a bit, unintentionally, I am tired with this last drink in my hand. And he staggers a bit, to show me I am not alone. He straightens and raises his shoulders. I can sleep. He will take it from here. He will write the note to be left on the countertop beside the coffeemaker. The one Love will read in the morning. I can handle the chores, I can lock the doors. I can make the coffee, he can add the spice. He will write the note that will make her smile and whisper my name tomorrow. I will have the face Love kisses tonight, I will have the armfuls and handfuls and caresses and touches for her. He will leave the words that are within me, the words my lips can not speak. He will leave them in the open light and air for the Morning to read and blush over. My soul, my bride, my best friend, she will read them with her sleepy eyes. I will crumble now, and I will dive. The platters will be full tomorrow, the banquet tables will be filled to bending. I will have the important and quiet things tonight, I will have the sultry things.

We have remade the room I was invited to enter years ago, and enter I did. The lights have been dimmed and the day retreats to lay outside the door. This is our sanctuary, this is where Love keeps all of her smiling faces. I will have my Love tonight, and the Poison Pen will spill all the words across the counter, they can crawl up the walls, they can take the ceilings. He and I part ways, and I am home, there are roselips, and no sadness to be found. There are nightlips, and no other sounds to be found.

DANCING

Morning is alive and elastic in our room, with all she brings and all she hides. She brings the lightest burdens to our luscious days. The heavier hours, the hours with weight and fight and teeth and knuckles, they seem to always come after. She may as well be a child jumping upon our bed. It doesn't seem like Love and I are the right age for children today. Last night is behind my ears and at the feet of my mind. The coffee will have to come in shovels, shovels and not spoons or cups.

My hands are not quite themselves yet, as I walk about opening the curtains, pulling them from the faces of each window I pass. Morning is already outside, she is giggling through her fingers. The day hasn't found its heat and there is activity all around like Christmas and I am pouring my first cup. I sigh into contentment and enlightenment, I'll keep a louder dirtier sigh for strangers, later. 'Is she here?' Love asks. And I laugh, yes, yes, Morning is outside, she is here whether the ground is wet or dry, and whether we are ready or not. She may be causing some trouble in the yard.

I will take my kiss but with only a half spoonful of sugar in my coffee. The brew is dark but not angry, I think I must have been in a hurry last night while preparing it. I must have been trying to get out of the way.

Love hums and drips her creamer and tells me she cherishes my notes. There will come a time she and I do not hear footsteps out here. Our yard is a luxury, our home gathers us in its arms, we sit in its lap, staring out into the hours waiting before us. She will work, I will work, but not yet. We will fashion ourselves and dress ourselves and steady ourselves into what the world will see. Morning dances around with filled baskets. The Day is looming, just over there, the sky is bringing it and the trees can not stop it, its face is right there on the waiting endless clock. It won't be too harsh, and it won't be too limiting, it may not be free and it may not be memorable, but it shouldn't be too demanding. We will find each other before its end, somewhere and sometime between here and there.

There is time before the first hardest edges of the day arrive. Love pulls her hand gently from mine and rises to water the pots and I stand with my cup and the memory of her hip. I can see, I can suddenly see. I see the new muses and their movements are delicate and delightful, they dance between the drops of water. They are each perfect in their way, perfect in their song, perfect in their purpose. 'I can see them', I say. Love has an arm soft at my back to answer, she knows I do. I hear no sound. And then the world groans. It has set its pillars, built its fences, it has voiced its limitations, but the new muses are here. Voices and pride will change, missions and paths will change, anger will be loud and doubt will be deafening, but as I am standing here, the muses are at my ankles. And I can finally see them.

They have arrived and will soon join their sisters. Life changes not with enormous greedy gulps and enormous greedy movements. But with subtle truths and trances that take years to recognize after the moments they are felt. The smoke and the hurry and the fury will disappear. The muses are candles in the daylight, they are freshness in the rain, they are the answers to the calls that rise in the loneliest minutes of the night. The muses come to surrender, they come to save. They come to relieve us from the shackles and the pain. The muses float and create, they hide, they sneak, they whisper and wait and seek and listen. They are the most gentle and most kind revenge against the cold and the empty.

They will be satisfied and be everlasting. And they will have all of us, the fortunate ones. I walk around the corner of our house. I see them, more colorful and vibrant than the roses they hide within. I am lost for a few moments, until I am found.

I walk across the patio, in search of another cup of coffee, I carefully step around Hope. She has her legs out in the sun. This is a day meant for dreaming and not working. We will do our part, Love and I. Love was my muse before there were maps drawn of the world. Love was my muse before I learned to speak or even stir. Love was my muse before all the ages. I have learned to be and leap and dance, I will sing and speak before I am done. Love is my muse, she has the chisels and pencils, Love is my muse, she has my heart and soul.

The honey resistance, and the spoils we experience every day. The water and the lovemadness and the lovewet all pool. We pull the posts and pull the fences to find the holes to let them gather. We are still discovering all the places we will grow. I feel the difference, I can now see the muses, and now some of the little things, the quiet things, may change their taste and color.

We have a bit more precious time before the day shows its teeth. Time for a couple more cups, time for some conversation with our forest of plants. There is no time for mischief, no time for cynicism. I am standing near Hope, she is enjoying the morning's warmth. She tells me she loves our landscaping. She appreciates Love's balance and purpose, she recognizes where I am allowed my taste for randomness and beautiful chaos. Hope tells me this all reminds her of a home she once built. 'Stay as long as you'd like,' I say.

Hope will always stay where she is embraced. She also seeks out the darkest corners where she has never been known. She seeks out the minds that are too afraid and too busy to dream, she seeks out the hearts that have only felt the heavy and the longing. Hope is fearless and tireless, a match for any of the other elements. She says she might sun the backs of her legs as well. I offer her a glass of lemonade, and when I return I give her one of Love's sun visors. Hope understands our lovespeak. When you drink with your eyes the light finds you, it makes its way through every crevice and crack. When you drink with your heart the light finds you, all the more. She stays a little longer, until her restlessness gets the best of her.

I move to kiss my bride of years and years, and she kisses me back. This is another moment we never want to leave. There is a stage filled with our moments, with the unique ones, the subtle ones, the glorious and well dressed ones. It grows and swells and everything harmlessly pours over the edges. We live in a world that can not contain our moments. We live in the luxury of our moments. Moments from last night and today, five years ago and five lifetimes ago, we wear them like pearls and fragrances and fine tailored suits, we wear them like long dances.

Love's feet are bare and wet, all the babies have been watered. I place a hand on her back, I want a kiss for yesterday, another for tonight, and another for tomorrow. I receive all three. I am awake and determined and unalarmed. Leave me lovelicked, our passion knows no limits, our passion knows no fear. It knows only comfort and creation. I want to just be us, for these last few hidden minutes. These are the minutes our unselfish greed wants to keep. These are the minutes that won't be part of the infestation.I pull a smile across her cheeks. She paints a smile across mine. This is the quiet life we want.

The clock is banging against the wall, it is demanding to be heard, it is screaming out the countdown. We both have what we must do today. The clock sounds off the minutes in a deepening voice. Yes, yes we know. There is a fire that is too hot, there is a fire that is too cold. There are fires with legs that must be caught. Let the rains fall, let the sun eat it all alive, let the moon twist, let the pages turn, let the truth jump out of the window to save itself. There are places our hands long to be. Let the prisoners out of their cages, let all the songs be performed and the movies be filmed. Let the cars drive in lines and the trains spill their goods. Let the flies bite and the predators hunt, let the news roll and the leaders learn to walk. I only need Love. In this bath. I only need memories and the memories we have yet to make.

The clock is so angry it is splitting in two, so I finally wander off to find my clothes for today. We will wear our working hands today. The meat must be cut and labeled and stacked high, the cleanings must be sparkling and perfect and perfumed and complete. There will be dollars, when it is all finished. But what I want more are our whispers in the dark. When it is finally over.

The labor may dress us, it will never define us. It does nothing to our wills. It can not change our smiles. Our dreams always outlast our obligations. Our dreams await our return, they are hungry when we return. I have seen foreign lands spread across maps, they speak of five day working weeks, they speak of two days of pleasure and leisure. They must be found over the bridge, they must be just out of sight and reach. Maybe just beyond the border. Perhaps we can reach these lands by raft, on a raft built for two. There is a reward out there, sometime and somehow. It will lead us back here, back home, back to the pleasantness, out of the shadows and into the cream. Out of the demanding and into the softness.

It is with a kiss, not a handshake, we survive the days. We thrive in our days, they ask for our meat and our bones and we decline. My Love and I, we do the twostep, we do the foxtrot. We survive the anklebiters and the shouldergrabbers. We make it home like wet avalanches, we make it home with softness and forgiveness. The drums of work will never be louder than the lovedrums. Our faces are never stolen during our days. We meet again, I know her and she knows me, and there is a hard truth within. She waits for me and I wait for her, and the words we long to hear, the words that press us through the day. The two words that separate us from the languishing and the insufferable. There are two words that dangle in the light, they wait to be spoken.

They push us past the petty and the ridiculous, they push us through exhaustion, they are a beacon, a promise.

My babe.

It is a simplicity that could tear the world in half. It is a simplicity that knocked my world over and made it complete. It embraces both the lost and the found. It nourishes, keeps us warm under the covers. There is no strategy or reason or motive. These words are a blush of brilliance, a call into the wild. My babe. They are a savage protest. They are a scent and a taste and a feel to keep my heart boiling and my soul churning and my mind spinning and my hands holding what can not be spent and can not be imprisoned. I want these words at the beginning and end of each day. When Love speaks them they burn through and through, they lift me, I shudder and understand all that is real and everything that is fantasy.

I know the difference between what momentarily collides with the eye and what is meant to hold. I know when the silence is stalled and broken, honesty is spoken and Love is there like an angel that can't be unfelt. She is dripping with devotion and I, too, am soaked. Throw a few words to me, like forever, my babe, throw a few words to me, like redemption, my babe. Throw a few words seeped in the luscious things, I will hear them and feel them.

Satisfaction is sitting heavy, heavy in my chair outside when I come home. He looks sunburned and tired, as though he has been waiting most of the day. I nod to him, no need to get up, I need to walk off the hours, I need to walk off the dust. I am over by the pots, the new muses are in neat little rows, they may be sleeping. Maybe they are waiting for Love, too. She will shower them when she comes home. I can not, I don't know the songs. We will all just wait, me and the muses and Satisfaction. I have left all the front doors open and wide, she will be here soon enough.

It is growing later, as the promise goes, we are beneath the moon and stars. Their silence is spilling down around us. There are no grievances or regrets, not here. Satisfaction has become heavier in my chair, his eyes have been closed for hours. I am happy to take off these clothes, I want to walk in the light between success and failure. If I dance as though I am crippled, she will know it is me, dancing.

Love tells me our bed is calling to her. I have but a little more in me, a little time in me. There is nothing to chew, nothing to ponder. The remains of the day will release me. There is a space within each evening, a space more than a minute or an hour. I stand in the wash. When the world is patient and hushed, I stand in the wash. Love is in bed, the trees are in bed, the noise is in bed, even the shadows are tired and laying on the ground.

The Legs are making their way across the grass, the Legs that know, the Legs that lead us to where we need to be. They may walk crooked sometimes, they may dance drunkenly sometimes, but they never fail. They are sturdy with trust, sturdy with devotion. They do not complain about the miles, they do not complain about the journey.

Sometimes they care too much, sometimes they speak too much. They bring us out of the darkness and the cold and the wet, they keep us safely out of the soup. The Legs are coming to tell me it is time to say goodnight.

It is time to kneel, it is never time to beg. It is time to remember there are only so many eyes in the world. It is time for a slow dance. A soul dance. There is nothing more to be said, there is nothing more to be heard. There is nothing more to be learned or forgotten. The Legs bring us to the touch, they bring us to the whispers. It is time to surrender to the soft places.

DREAMING

It is a rare morning and I remember my dreams from last night. I see snarled and ravaged pieces of them. They are hanging on me, my eyes feel sandy. They give the world a hint of beige and gray. Remembering my dreams can throw my steps off, at times, it is my left, lagging a bit, not keeping its dance with my right. The dreams lasted through the night, they grew like choking vines. I haven't had such dreams in a long time, I had hoped they would never find me again.
They were top heavy, clumsy dreams, stumbling falling frustrating dreams, my mind and my body would not listen, they could not agree. I sat up countless times in the night, I would try to rub my face clean of them, I would rise and try to walk myself free of them. They waited for me like a mouth. They would not release me. I know I struggled, I vaguely

recall being told to turn on my side. I know I tried to escape, Love tried to quiet my walking legs. I know the dreams were horrific, I squeezed her hand too tightly.

I dreamed of the wicked, and my arms and shoulders are trying to shake the sensation. This feel of them, I don't want it in my hair and around my eyes and throat. I am pacing as though I am trying to leave. I keep heating my coffee and forgetting it is in my hands. I dreamed of places I never intend to find. I am telling my hands to forget, I am telling my guts and my heart to forget. The dreams are persistent cobwebs and the spiders keep running. I have to convince myself I am safe, I am here.

I don't remember the faces, I don't remember the voices. I dreamed of the Sirens, they are a wax across this morning. I dreamed of the Sirens, never knowing who or what they are. I dreamed they launched themselves from their hiding places, they erupted from their deepest, violent pools. And the madness they inspired and the chaos they created. Their victims were strung up like lights with empty eyes and opened mouths. I dreamed through a storm so sudden even the Elements were taken by surprise and helpless to stop it. There were too many humanity fires burning at once. I dreamed of the Sirens, they are an oil on this morning.

It was a massacre of the senses, an unprovoked war. The Sirens awakened and wanted their prizes. I dreamed men fell, one by one, by temptation or force. They were unprepared, they hadn't the means for defense or retreat. Or perhaps not the will.

'You were dreaming all night,' Love says. Yes, and I will have to find some strength in this day, I will have to find some strength in its light. I have to find the direction again, the ambition, because I am swollen with the dreams. I have the ache of being half awake and half lost. The Sirens never came for me with their filthy hands and loose tongues and loose dresses. I never heard their calls. They just wanted me to witness.

Love is wearing something light and flowing for the heat of August. I am trying to get my feet beneath me. I know it is not the Night that lingers, she flows and caresses us and then sets herself free. I sense a callousness and a danger that does not belong here. Our bed is unmade and our house is still mostly undressed. I wander into the yard, maybe looking for a promise. I want some pressure, some pulse, to take the dreams away. I wait for the gentle ease to make me climb from this state and return to where I want to be. Love is pulling out the hoses. She is speaking tenderly and the muses are finally appearing through the petals.

'I heard the muses whimpering last night,' Love says. I did not. I was locked in a dream I feel was not mine. Love is showering everything she reaches, the roses are dancing, the muses are dancing, the air is lightening, my steps are becoming more themselves. Perhaps with more dancing, with some water and some food, the agitation will disappear, and we'll find ourselves back in the heat. The day will discover we have no plans and so much to do. This is the ease of the days with Love, these are the hours that sneak past my soul. The are the simple days that become promise and dedication.

I adore her bare feet, the way they tap, and the way they chase away the worries. I love her in this dress, it takes my mind away. I give her the second real kiss of the day. It's a kiss that has never known starvation or wait. I kiss her with a taste of longing. I kiss her with a hundred year kiss. And here we are. The lines and the ropes are falling from today and we are floating freely.

The assaulting Sirens were but a dream to be forgotten. They have no courage or strength here, no matter their imagined numbers, their imagined ferocity. Love wants to dig some holes today and feed the earth some flowers. This is our happy kingdom, we are queen and king, we are gardeners for the day, fools for the night. The hummingbirds are laughing with the new little muses, the butterflies are offering them tickling rides. One more cup of coffee should do the trick. I can see no storms on the horizon. I feel no storms on the horizon. I am returning to a dream these hands can taste and feel.

The roses are in full dress today in reds and pinks I can not describe. They twist in the breeze and dip and rise in yellows and oranges, lavenders and whites. The older muses take refuge in the shade, they are not as reckless or adventurous as the new. The sun is a brutal early riser today, it is stirring and simmering the pot to a boil. It wants to be fierce today. It can be as it wishes today. Yesterday was a little gaunt, with the working hours. Today will be overflowing.

The shovel is readied with its first strikes, the ground never howls and never protests. We sink the roots deep. Each addition is another step towards the vision. Our peaceful paradise tucked within the folds of the village. It's a splash of color and a flash of beauty which may go unnoticed by some or most. But, oh, how it calls to us. It is our reward, our reward we earn each day, after a suffered wait, after a brief spiritual chill. We have shed their hands and shed their voices. I see now Awareness has come.

Awareness appears, hunched like a predator with unbelievable strength and a growl filled with teeth. You know once he has you. Love and I have long since forgotten the initial shock and terror. It lasts but an instant. He does not seek to devour, he does not wish to pull you to the depths, he doesn't plan to drag you away to his nest. Awareness has a grip that is terrible, and then immediately comforting. He wants only to hold you, experience you, and then illuminate you. Once in his jaws the feel of his teeth disappears, he dresses you warm or wet, however it is needed, he offers blankets and fires, cold washes and drinks. Once Awareness has secured and rescued you, you are the one to walk, you are the one to lead, he is there but to follow and gently remind.

And then the dark days fade and you begin to understand his whispers and how he bends the light.

Suddenly you are no longer walking, not kneeling and not surrendering, you are floating and climbing. Awareness wants to surround you and set you free. He wants to hear the words when you decide you are more than your struggles. He wants to stand beneath you as you rise. Love and I had many chapters and many years and lives to be cleansed of. Awareness is a wonderful painter, his colors taste of liberation. Awareness is also a wonderful partner as we complete our kingdom chores. He performs no labor, no digging, no carrying, no sweating. He sighs and approves. I believe he sees us more as children than as the rescued. We wear our faces the same as he does, in the sun or in the rain, we wear them above our shoulders and above our hearts, out in front of our spirits.

There has been a carnival of distractions and interruptions today, but the afternoon is pleasant and still lingering. It is lounging with one leg over the rooftop and the other over the neighbors' fence. Love and I pause for a moment to survey what we have done. There is a new press of colors spilled across the ground. We worked with no demands and no deadlines, we worked lovingly and fiercely and passionately and leisurely. The beautiful sweat is upon our brows. There is a time to stop and a time to continue, a time to carry it all inside, there is a time to rest and a time to quietly appreciate all we have done. We agree we have changed the world again, our small part of it. We are humbled and satisfied and thirst, and I suggest the shade that is softening the edges in front of the trees.

These are the lost hours that are irreplaceable and undeniable. We enjoy them, we horde them, they are treasures, they are unkept and unruly and lovedefined. These are the pursued hours, the precious hours, the lovepossessed hours. We walk hand in hand towards the very edge of what we call our own. We stand beside what we believe in, we stand within what we know. We sit together in chairs to capture a new perspective of lovecarnage we create.

Happiness nearly takes us by surprise, she is up on a branch like a cat. She laughs and waives. She is too pretty and too sweet and too young to possess such weapons. She wasn't lurking, she was eavesdropping. She wasn't spying she was contributing. I am too relaxed to tell her to be careful up in that tree. But then Happiness should never be cautious or careful. She seeks heights and dances around the moon, she reminds us of places we want to be. Happiness has her carriages and horses and her long lined entourage, she has her fireworks and her subtle sleepy times. She is not intrusive, she is light as a feather. She likes to play with the pieces of the luscious things.

It is possible, now, the day's patience has worn thin, though I don't think with us, but the world at large. It may be weary from the way the world moves back and forth, heavy and relentless, like a machine, a rolling pin. Maybe it is time to take our place inside. The hours offered to us have been thoroughly lovechoked. They are laying contentedly all around us. There is a hint in Love's eyes, there is a song in my voice. I think we can squeeze the mystery and see what comes. We are a little light and a little hungry, we are a little ravenous and soaked with content. I hold Love's hand all the way to the door. We are going to let the world stay outside our walls and windows tonight. We are going to let our eyes and hands have what they see and roam freely.

Should the inheritance from your father be offered in the form of work ethic, you can flee screaming from it or embrace it. I chose soaking consumption of it. There are times it seems I have extra working hands, six, even seven of them, though my lovehands can number more. There are times I feel him smiling at me. There are days I would prefer to be home, expanding our english garden. There are days I would prefer to be home, watching the truth trickle through the grass and into the pools. There are days when the clouds don't feel so high, days I feel I can do something. And this is one of them.

But I heed the call, I have the endurance. I make the effort, countless times I push against the swinging door at the butcher's shop. I tell the meatcutter we are winning, but I wonder if we ever are. Someone has released the masses, they shuffle like trolls, like zombies, they are uncoordinated, maybe confused. There is a writhing wall of humanity just outside the coolers. The meat rolls out in towering, teetering racks, it rolls out in barrels and in fistfuls, any and every way possible. We've got our knuckles in it, our elbows in it, we sing and cuss and laugh, just to keep getting the meat out to the faces.

Meat to the hungry and happy faces, meat to the angry and impatient. Meat to the familiar faces from the village, meat to the faces of the coming storm of visitors. Meat to the small and the tall, meat to the poor and the rich. All of us, down to the last man, are dogged by the years and the efforts, chased by the paths which lead us to this room. You can almost hear them over the radio. Maybe those in the warmth outside say a little prayer that the cold may preserve the undefeated men inside. Sometimes it is the back or the feet, sometimes it is our own hands that try to betray us. There is no quit or pause. You take time for a powder, or a couple minutes out of the cooler's grip.

We will be paid and paid fairly, it will reach our hands and we can hold it for a moment, and now pay for everything else. It is not forever, it is a challenge, one that is issued and accepted. We all found our way to the butcher's shop, and we come by our own free will. Three or four men, we all wait until the last song of the dance is played. We want to hear the silence when it is over. The goal is to exit, being the same man who entered. The number of hours and the strain matters little. It is easily forgotten once the doors are closed behind us. Three or four men in a village of thousands, returning to our wives and our homes and our lives. It is the meat dance, the meat parade, there is no glitter or glamour, we go now to satisfy our own appetites.

The obligations are gorged and fulfilled, I'll allow the evening to come as it wishes and later expire as it will. I am walking off the fatigue, I am walking off the chill. My muscles and bones are becoming my own again. The day gets left in a heap of my clothes. It is always this way. I return to freedom and peace. I wander outside, I notice splashes and surprises of color that were not there just yesterday. I hope Love comes home soon, it is her hands that are all over this world and this life I know. The ground reminds me of her steps, her laughter is in the bushes, her songs are within the riches. I am comfortable, knowing how uniquely fortunate I am. I am comfortable, I dropped to my knees long ago and was raised to my feet.

At the farthest reach from our home, in the tallest grasses, I encounter Lovecandy. She leaps the short gate which hides our little bridge. 'It's okay, there is no one else here,' I say. Lovecandy never comes around and never stays when the other Elements can be found. She relaxes for a moment, she wants to know what I am doing, she always wants to know what we are doing. I tell her I am just waiting, she says she knows, I am always waiting, she says it almost like a child, she says it with an I told you so tone and feel.

Maybe I am waiting, maybe I am wishing, there is thin whisper of a difference between the two. She leaps back over the fence. We can wait and wish together. She is one of Love's favorites, they always embrace like old friends. She has unabashed innocence. Lovecandy has the eyes of a burglar, a voice of a songbird, thighs like thunder, and a heart and soul dripping with loyalty.

She gets startled and tells me the Sticky is here. I hear Love come outside through the backdoor. I turn to her and smile, I turn around and Lovecandy is gone. Love asks me through a kiss how my day was, and I finish my brief walk at her side. The only answer I can find is 'Better now.'

I know Lovecandy was right, and she always is in sudden moments and bursts. Love and I are outside where we belong with the night upon our skin, our days are sleeping dogs at our feet. There are surely planets somewhere above us and dreams all around us. The Sticky seeps over us like honey, it keeps the lovespiders and their webs from running away. It feels our passion and decides to take a swim. It listens without speaking and cheers for the crackles and groans as our souls collide and reconnect like continents. It tastes our truth like salt, our fever like sugar. The Sticky drapes and mauls like nothing else can.

It is self conscious about its girth and careful with its power. I smile to tell it we are right here and we are all just fine. The Sticky tells us what we have is never far from what we want, we are ever so close. It blurs the sky and covers the ground and asks if we are ready for it to put us to bed. We wish for a little more time, some more of this sweetness of this later hour. And it dances back from us as if we were hot candles. The Sticky will always find us, in the tightest and loosest spaces.

The Sticky keeps the shards and ashes away, it keeps the smoke and the distractions away. We are always within its reach, Love and I. It keeps salvation from screaming so loud, it shows salvation the path, and we are all in the thick of it. We are all in this together. It knows how we trust, it knows we dance differently the closer it gets to midnight. Love and I, salvation, the passion and the purpose, we've all got our clothes on, the Sticky makes certain of it. It softly warns us, the world outside is up on its elbows and knees, it is ready and searching for an obnoxious and frivolous late night. We are turning off the lights and locking all the doors. Our modest little home for two has beaten us to it, it is comfortable and still and fast asleep.

The dreams were persistent last night, they were raw, I was trapped by them again. They are but scattered silent images now, dismay and discomfort painted in black and white. The Sirens possessed the meek and the feeble, they chased the righteous through the streets. The dreams hang wet, the dripping aftermath of a vicious nightstorm. They are beginning to fade and dry. The sun is blazing, the ground is parched. Two of my favorite blossoming plants were knocked over. I peer down into them and see the new muses have their eyes clenched tight. They are not sleeping, they are not playing.

We are all waiting for a little rain, a little forgiveness. The Morning serves as the conductor for the day, she determines its length and its course, its feel and its taste. She positions it and releases it. I do not yet understand her plans for this one. I do not understand her purpose for adding outside noise to this day. There is some restlessness and some recklessness, some anxiety Love and I do not associate with and do not recognize as our own.

Nothing ever comes between us, nothing ever draws us apart. And the Morning is aware of this, she relishes it. The newness of old souls freed and then joined. Old souls in a single kiss and a single touch. I do not know why the Morning has decided to play and compromise with confusion, I will give no weight to these terrible coincidences, this is nothing I can fix with my own hands. I can feel all the chores I have chosen for today are waiting for me, they are in piles, they are watching me. I can't seem to start and I can't envision the finish. I need help with this day. That which is within my control was intended to be quiet. Love will join me later, but now there is an unfamiliar sense of feeling small against the world. As though I must find the keys, find the strength and the will. This is all foreign, this is new to the man who bears my name.

I could use a little assistance, a bit of direction away from what I can only assume feels like weakness. There is a ripple of movement, a sudden tone of delight, out of earshot and barely in my line of vision. It is Peace within the splendor of another of her grand entrances, Peace in her flowing gown and in her gentle ways. I feel I need some relief from these conflicting reflective thoughts, I feel as though I could use some of her forgiveness and her permission. I hope I am the type of man who may ask for such things. Peace has made her way closer, effortlessly, soundlessly. She smiles at me as though I am a man who does not have to plead with her. I am a man who will be asked for nothing in return. Peace grants me both forgiveness and permission, I assure her I will take nothing more and expect nothing more. Her whispers tell me I will receive all that I need.

For those of us who live in her wake, whose lives unfold tracing her steps, who exist just beyond her gentle pushes, Peace actually follows us. She guides us from the cliffs, she keeps us off the rocks. She is tranquil and unburdened and unassuming, she walks beside us and speaks to us. Her touch is a force, her wisdom is offered without words. Peace is never frail, she never ages, she is subtle and deafening. She will never struggle here, not while Love and I are here. She has a safe place to wonder and wander, she has a safe place to rest. 'Do you see how easy that was, Leo?' she says.

My eyes are reopened, my heart is fresh, I am awake, I am myself, and things appear exactly as they should be. The heat has relented, the questions have relented, I have been surrounded by lightness and freedom. The Day quickly and quietly finds its place and rests and allows me to walk through it. I promise I will be gentle and easy, I promise my mind has found its way again.

The unrest has returned to its slumber, the difference between labor and lovetoils are the lovenudges, and I will satisfy my hunger for those today. My every movement seems to be relieved of effort. I feel strength and resilience returning. I accomplish nothing for a higher purpose today, the ground seems to groan in ecstasy, the gardens seem to welcome her new companions. I am whispering as Love does, trying to speak gently to the roots, reassuring them they will like it here. I am a dirt champion, I am a lover and a kisser, I am a meat poet, I am a groom waiting for his lovely lovely bride.

The chores I piled are shrinking and crumbling and beginning to fade. They were chores by name alone. They are lovemovements. I pause, feeling I have built castles. The breezes blow through them, they are dancing, I am evolving, I am learning. The sky doesn't seem to know what to do with itself, it now hangs deep heavy clouds above my shoulders. It can do as it wishes. I have lived that simple life today, I have lived a life of dreams. I am a man who received forgiveness and permission to taste some of the luscious things.

Today has been meat and bread for the heart and the soul. As good as the earth feels beneath my feet, I decide to take a break at the tables and chairs in the coolest, pleasant part of the yard. The shade is fine, the sun doesn't speak, and the perspective changes. There is nothing around my ankles and wrists. It's though I am looking towards the known, from beyond, I am looking into the known, perhaps upside down. This is what other eyes see. I am two delicious beers closer to telling the tools they have reached the end of their working day. I am thirty minutes into this chair and that much closer to when Love and her eyes will be home.

I hear footsteps that sound like old friends are approaching. The Sparks has come again, he likes to splash, he likes to burst in for visits, he always appears hot and certain and confident. The Poison Pen is just behind him because he likes his drinks too much and he knows what a late afternoon with The Sparks involves. I welcome them both and we laugh loudly and carefree. The Sparks arrive unannounced and randomly as always, he takes his spot at the table and drops his jug to hold between his feet. He slaps my back and tells me I have always been one of his favorites, and then asks if I ever used that lure, used that line he gave me. He takes a long drink from his jug and winks at me and asks about my pretty wife.

'She is more beautiful and breathtaking every day,' I say. The Poison Pen asks for another and then takes two, he is already three to my one. To make things cloudy and slow them down so he can capture the flow, capture the words. He stands and staggers and then imitates how I was dancing the last time out in the night. We all roar with laughter, The Sparks takes two enormous gulps from his jug and rises from his chair. As unsteady as the Poison Pen is with his leaps and lunges, The Sparks has a fierce look and demeanor, a once in a lifetime demeanor, a right now edge, a must be you look. His expression says he has got to shake some moves for his lady, he stammers, he can not be late. But then he halts his rush, he pauses and calms, he smiles, 'You give my best to Love,' he says.

The Sparks raises his collar high around his neck and shrugs his belief that he is quite suave and debonair. He throws another wink. The Poison Pen will stay until the drinks are gone. We sit at the table and stare at each other wondering how can it be, with these faces of ours, the words will come and become. Yet here we are in the humidity and now the light rain, squeezing the final drops. The Poison Pen suggests a filthy note tonight, I hand him the last can, and remind him this was a day of a softness and a forgiveness. He staggers away a bit, into the calm of the trees.

I make my way through the yard, I have my feet up in the clouds but they are coming in earnest, now, they are coming in armies, they are coming with shouts, explosions. I can see Love spilling through the windows inside. I am trying to make the short walk, through the gray, everything from ten minutes ago is being washed through the grass. The rain is soaking now. I make it to the back door, Love hands me a towel and a smile. 'Old friends?' she says. Yes, old friends, old wet friends. I kiss her to celebrate the way we are home together, the way we can be apart and together, the way we bend in and out of this space.

I kiss her to celebrate our lover's reunion and our lover's ritual and our lover's reasoning. We can enter a moment and nothing can touch us. There is no map or math or graph for us, there is no studied cure. We are lovestruck and lovestretched and lovebound. We have to take out the trash and push it past the aches of the day. Her shoulders feel just like my knees. Without speaking, we agree to an unremarkable night tonight, we agree to lay beyond a plain closed door. We agree to get lost in the rain and fade beyond the light. We are locked in a trance, we are locked in steps of an excruciating endless terrible dance. Our moves improve and it only gets worse. The handyman and the cleaning lady, the butcher and the pretty pretty bulldog. I hope we remain anonymous in our village. I hope we are a passing pleasant breath. We have hands that do and hands that create. We have hands that never steal or strike. We have lips for speaking and lips for adventure, lips for the calm and the in, lips for the wild. Sometimes we can tire, between what we know and what we dream. But it takes just the sudden blue shock of Love's eyes. Evolution presents itself on a cold plate. The meat is what we make, the meat is what we take as our own. The rest is what we will no longer eat and no longer endure. Love sets the evening table and I want to lay across it.

My eyes are casting light nets across this pleasant evening. I feel like I am waiting. Love's voice lingers through the walls, she tells me she knows. She knows the fabric and fashion of my soul, she knows my heart and my heart's delights, and I know hers. She knows my mind must empty just as it feeds. Love is laying out the dishes and I am lingering and starving and still waiting for the relief and the release. Every day has a tale, and every day must be finished. The sweatbox must be emptied, the heat must be released. It is the only way we can lay together. The feast must eat. This day will lose its words soon. And Love will be waiting with her own.

Everything that can run fast enough will not be emptied. Everything that is felt can not be torn. I want to pull our walls in tight, the Night and the world are invading. I want our truth and our fever to block out even the hunger and the lights. Our patience will outlast Pleasure's jittery hands. There is some freedom left and we will find it, we will tidy it all up tomorrow. We can take what it ours from the silence and the friction, we can take what is ours from the thick and the shouts. We will make bricks of it all, we will have ours yesterday, today, and tomorrow. They can't have what we have, Love, it can't be taken and it can't be sold. Ours is a mystery found with fingers and whispers, and perhaps ours does not make sense to the primitive and the educated, but it can't be stolen, it must be possessed.

Tonight has some legs and arms that crave us, and if they don't use us up, they will spill us into tomorrow. If they don't like our taste, we will survive another week, we will survive again. It is the way we hang and do not fall. We are the gossip and the lust and the gravy.

I can hear Envy rolling his heavy dumpsters around. It's a clammering, they are sad noises in the distance. He has his treasures and pleasures, and the stink is almost unbearable. I wish he would just be off on his journey. He can drift through another yard and another time. He can find an accomplice, he can find another ear to speak to. He can change someone else's eyes and change someone else's face. Our time is endless, and we have no room for him. Our time is priceless and he offers no baits or enchantments. Not here. Love has dragged her soul and will through our door, and I will drag mine.

There is the cream and the kisses and everything delicious. Envy offers the hollow shadows and the lifesick desires. I will never jump or shiver or shudder. I will never leap towards what he may bring, singing his sad songs, spraying his wares, pulling at his own offerings. I haven't a single thing I would be crushed to do without. I am blind to his eyes, I am deaf to his suffering. What Love and I share comes in buckets and blankets and long, long stories and laughter. I will climb the mountains within me. I will reach the heights Love lays before me. Not as a test. But as a pinch of forever.

Tonight, tonight, I want our lovepiles at the windows, I want our love seeping into the carpets. I want our gestures and promises to press the ceiling. I want our love to invade the dark and drown out the lights. I want privileged, secret, sacred love. I want heaving adoration that splashes the walls and the covers and devours and smothers us. I want to be gasping for air and receive none.

Tonight, I want the doors shut and the eyes closed, I want the sheets dripping shamelessly to the floor. I want no questions beneath the bed and no answers from the silence. There will be no thirst or hunger, there will be just us and all the unmentionable moments. Tonight, I want to be alive, tonight I need Love's arms and legs, tonight I need her voice and all she releases and all she causes. I want to wait and I want to hurry.

Tonight, I want all the subtle and sultry things, I want in her safety and explosions. I want to wear the uniforms of lovers. I want Love simple and complicated, daring and demure, I want her to be weary and relieved. We can shout through the lovemadness. We will lovedrench the dry and the sickly. Lovefeet will bounce out the lazy and nearly dead. Her voice is stout and loud in my ears, her voice is in my throat. The stale and pale simply disappear, they have no place here. I am lovebathed, I am lovehungered and quenched. It will keep the dreams at bay. I am washed, I am emboldened, we will dance tonight. I want to have this bed without the weight of dreams tonight, just her arms, just her kisses.

We have left our footprints at the door so it can't be opened, we leave our delights in the air so we can't be surprised. The lovestench is thick, so thick we can't hear the traffic, we can't hear the storms, we can't hear the hours. The day is gone and this night is long and taken into Love's hands. There is too much paint, too much gravy, the slick is astonished when it turns to steam. Nothing else can possibly be. Not in this room, not within this closeness, not in this humidity, in this tired, tired night. The success rolls across in waves and blankets, the success plays trumpets.

There is space but for our own swollen spilling hearts, our greedy grasping hands and lips. We are dazed and battered with wounds to keep us safe in the dark until morning. I look upon Love's blushed face, I look into her kept eyes. The way we will sleep, no one would ever know there are two in this room, two above the fray and the struggle, two who ripped through the fabric, two in the depths and the throes. We hold tighter in this luscious avalanche.

KNOWING

I stand admiring a raw morning with a raw first cup in my hand. I have no memories of dreams from last night. I have nowhere to be today and I am waiting for my mind to open to the possibilities. They will come, slow and sure. Things have chosen to be quiet and quick today. It is a mild, unintrusive day. A day a working man might consider a reprieve. A day an overly anxious and overly ambitious man might consider an opportunity, or a failure. So far, I like the warmth of the coffee against my hands.

I see Envy has stayed all night, just at the edges, just on the outside. He slept on top of one of his dumpsters. I hope he was rained on, I hope he was cold and regretted staying, I hope he was miserable. He was going to receive no welcome here. I am feeling a bit soft and drifting today, as though my thoughts are being choked inward.

Generosity comes in with a leap, he shows me his hands, I watch them form into a shove. He is pushing the dumpster, pushing with all his might, he is straining to move it from my sight. I'll cook him breakfast, if he succeeds, I'll wash the dishes. My hands are big enough, my heart is rich enough. I can help. Generosity's efforts aren't worldly appreciated, but I thank him, for moving that stinking dumpster out of my view. He has told me it is not the depths of our pockets, it is not our wealth, it is the honesty and simplicity. The desire to give to all. Love comes outside and Generosity waives and blows her a harmless kiss.

'Did you sleep at all last night?' she says. And I thought I must have, but now I consider this heavy, heavy head I carry around. I think she looks beautiful this morning and she thinks I am quite handsome, so this day has some legs beneath it, it has some wind behind it. Generosity bids us good day, I wonder about the pleasure of having more, having more but not all, having more freedom to give it away. I want a life knowing the giving chills and the giving shudders. I want the charitable warmth, the humanitarian warmth. I want a life where I experience the pleasure of release, over and again, the happiness of my own becoming the happiness of another.

Love asks if I hear her and if I will rest today. I will take my own version and burden of rest, and yes, I always hear her. She awoke to the screams of the muses last night, she went outside with only her shoes and a flashlight. The burrowing eyes of Worry were pressing on her through the darkness, and she had to come back inside. I have not made it far enough around our house to see the signs of the chaos. Love is straightening and standing the flowerpots, she is watering each as she goes. I can't hear her through the wetting showers but I can see her face. The dreams of the

Sirens were silenced last night, but their vandalism seems real.

Love wanders and consoles, she whispers, she tells the muses their river is gone, it is no longer there. The muses see her and hear her and trust her and seem to calm. There may be a reason to run, but they have no other hiding places. Love wants me to tell them we will keep them safe. I am speaking to her and the muses, I offer my back, I offer my arms, I offer my strength and persistence, my endurance and stubbornness. We are all in each other's hands, it seems, whether for now or eternity.

I do not care to have Worry rummaging around our house, especially at night, with Love wandering in the darkness. It has been a long time since I have wept into his yellow eyes and stomped my feet into forgiveness. He gives you shallow promises and longhearted neglect. He comes with a banquet to make you feel as though you are starving. He comes to drown and consume you. Worry knows nothing of where you have been, he knows nothing of what you are capable of doing. He wants his hand at the back of your head as you are trying to keep your nose out of the water. He wants his hands on your shoulders as the lions approach. Worry will capture your breath and blame it on the wind, he will blame it on yesterday and tomorrow. He will hold your hips and make you angry instead of dancing and leaping. He will suck and steal the lush from the lusciousness.

I kiss Love for last night, I kiss her for today. I kiss her for her tenderness and the way she makes the sky blush.

I kiss her for the casual closeness, I kiss her for the forever ride. I kiss her for disguising herself in this dress and I will always remember her wearing it for a couple hours on a Tuesday. Love kisses me back, because she knows and remembers, we drip with it and we stink with it, we walk with it and can't escape from it.

We are two found souls in a flame we embrace more than we understand. We would rather feel than know. The Elements are free to roam and foam across our backs and lay upon our shoulders, they are free to roam and foam around our steps. They won't hear and they won't dictate the next words I say to her. Love takes my hand for a long, long delicious moment. This is the juicy and the salty, the have and the had, the rushing moments and the movements forward. This is the absolute calm of where we are. Hidden, in the darkness, hidden, in the light, this is what we have discovered, and this is all we know. I am rich with stories I will tell Love in secret languages, and she is rich with reactions to tell me she knows exactly what I am saying.

Some mornings are like this, most mornings are like this. Love and I find ourselves in a state of being. We are ourselves, we have no desire to chase into other people's corners. Love draws close to my side and gathers my hips and my legs and gathers my arms. These moments of perfection. This is where the hush is in our hands. This is where the future stands just before us. This is when I wish Generosity would spread his tools. I would like to share this, this and everything else. Except the fever between us.

74

It is as though a smile you asked for has been seen and you see it every time as the first time. Your heart does not wonder, and it does not wander, it is home. Your soul is not crushed, it is burning itself alive, it wipes the corners of your mouth, it wipes the words you can not speak, it wipes at the tastes you dare.

'I love you, Leo' is the only song I can take. I am brought to my knees, I am brought to my proudest, strongest moments. I have an angel who carries me with her wings. I have an angel who makes me reach into the night and reminds me I am just where I need to be.

How quickly the day seems to have surrendered those legs it was threatening to run upon. It has taken on a bloated feeling, a laziness, an attitude of entitlement. It may not want a memory, it may be laying down in tomorrow's hands. This day has crumbled off the path. It has lost its direction and discarded its interest. And the weather senses it, the weather feels its opportunity to take control. It rolls across the world as though it is on wheels. The winds have met the clouds and they are fighting. The rain comes in angry angles.

I am not selfish, I am right to say we live in a kingdom. Today my rule is reduced to a garage, the doors are opened wide, the air inside is close and crawling, the winds stop throwing it once inside. I am spilling secrets, I am letting the world know I am home. The walls are sweating, though it seems it is just me here alone, with the flies. There is enough room to breathe, to stand and sit and pace. There is little activity to be found. There are scattered tools at hand but nothing to build.

I can push everything aside and lose this afternoon to remembering and forgetting. I can offer some hours to calm dreaming. Or I can have some drinks with the Poison Pen. From the back door, I can see him standing beneath the cover of an enormous branch of an enormous tree. He does not like being wet. In this moment, we are both realizing, what we can do can be simplified. It can be explained, it can be called waiting. We can ignore the rumors of the respectable hour. I look inside the refrigerator, there is enough for me, and enough to quench the appetite of the Poison Pen. I return to the back door with an icy can in my hand and raise it as an invitation. I raise it as a toast. He raises his hand in return. We are in agreement, we are the type of men which find the soft rules and the etiquette look the other way.

The Poison Pen makes his way across the yard, it looks like a stiff wind could knock him over. But he is steady, for now. From a distance we might pass as brothers. He comes in out of the rain. One for our bones, I insist, and he suggests one for our blood, one for our meat, another for our brains, one in each fist. And so it goes, and this is how this day will be stretched. I know when the coaxing is over, when the comradery is finally wet, he will leave. And he will leave a note in a mischief tongue for Love to find, and I won't mind the way he speaks to my wife. He has a lightness and a bit of clever to him, he must be in my mind. Because there are times she kisses me sweet for no reason.

These are the last soggy hours of the afternoon, and they are going to lay on me splendid, they are going to lay on me with some gentle hands. I realize the difference between knowing and not knowing is but a sliver, a light. It is a genuine accident, it is a whisper. Knowing the walls are not closing, knowing they aren't interested enough to listen. Knowing I may bend, knowing some steps do not take.

Some years get washed and some years become memories, some years are madness and some years are too cold to grip. Some years are dry and stagnant, some are nothing more than placeholders. Some years are dizzy with evolution, some are larger than they are supposed to be. Some years are monstrous, they unleash volcanoes, they tread across the waters. Some years shovel the heaps of the wreckage and the rest, they grab your attention, they make you belong. They convince you with kisses, they convince you with sweet caresses. Some years find you when you are not hiding anymore. I find myself misty and humbled and comfortable, not missing the years I have lost, bathing in the years I have gained. Knowing I am gorged upon the years with Love.

The afternoon has become so heavy it lays on the floor and I have to walk around it. Knowing without having the answers, knowing without having doubts. I realize I know about the muses, and the Sirens, with perhaps more intimacy than I care to have. Knowing is a possession, it can be a reason or a weapon. It could shatter this silence, but I have no one to speak to until this evening.

The truths can be seen in the air and heard in the very soil. The Sirens ooze and writhe and have worldly needs, the muses seek the power of one heart, one soul. The Sirens lured us and feasted upon us until there were not enough sailors, the muses gently ache and wait to be called. There is no drift into the fog, knowing the difference between the wet and the wildness and the ravenous appetites, as opposed to the contentment and enlightenment.

Over the centuries, the Sirens' need for seduction became hungrier and more difficult to satisfy. It was no longer enough to lure young adventurers and smash them upon the rocks. They had to come into the farms and towns, and then they had to come into the cities. The Sirens' march knew no boundaries. Their skills sharpened, their teeth and claws sharpened. They learned to sing their songs through clouds, and we were damp with them before we could even beg or struggle. They came to the lands of concrete and glass, they came to their ultimate hunting grounds. They preyed upon us, beckoning us from offices and vehicles, from supermarkets and homes and churches. They stalked us down dark alleys and lit streets, they stalked us in broad daylight. We tasted sweet in moments of loneliness and weakness, we tasted sweeter still in moments of confidence and passion.

It seems dreaming has become knowing, the visions at night can linger in my mind by day. The Sirens live in a limited universe. They exist within a frenzy of destruction, a frenzy of gratification. The hunt lasts longer than the feast, hunger and thirst will return. What eludes them always is true satisfaction. The holes are slowly consuming them, they rage and try to fill them, will them with lust and power and deception.

The muses have a gentle, limitless existence. A purity the universe does not seek to crush or contain. They are fed by dreams and hopes, they offer inspiration, they offer clarity and fulfillment. They offer what is beyond the reach and the abilities of a manmade world. The muses know only what is meant to be. They patiently wait until it is recognized. They live in peace until the blind can see and the voiceless can sing. They are not possessed, they are not deceived, they know nothing of tricks or wealth, of status or class. Each muse knows their own warmth and light and they wait for the whisper.

A muse longs for a single soul to be awakened. It can take years, it can take lifetimes, and the muses are not troubled. Their purpose is soul to soul, soul upon soul, soul within soul. They know nothing of loss or grief, they never learn the meaning of disappointment. Simplicity and calm surrounds them. Their intended place, their destined world, has a voice, has a face. Oh, but when a muse is finally discovered, when a muse is finally invited, that place, that world, will be forever altered. It will begin to exist.

The Sirens enjoy the feel of the fashionable, the scent of the successful, the aftertaste of the righteous. The muses are not confined or defined, they are not here for the artists, they are not here for the creators. A muse is unique, it is meant for one and only the one. What the one does with their hands and their mind and their time makes no difference. It is the uncontrollable eternal call. The Sirens' way is an undefinable sickness, it is an inhumane wound. It is a relentless dance with no pleasure. They despise the muses with a feel and a burn. Perhaps they despise Love and I, too.

A muse needs but a moment, a glance, a wish, a word. A muse does not create life, it stops the linger, it stops the hunger, it awakens a life. My sweet Love is an old, old muse, I lived long without her. I lived many times, I lived as though I actually existed, as though I may have mattered, I lived without being alive. One day I might describe it, the saturation, the embrace, the comfortable longing, the simple pleasure and the ecstasy, the calm alluring devouring fever. The known and the unknown. We were perhaps halfway into the story, we were discovered and will never escape it. It does not demand, it does not call our names.

Love and I glow with it, our hearts will never again be worried or fragile, our hearts will never again be misled or assaulted, silenced or neglected. We are thankfully recklessly taken. We are two, accounted for, we are two planted and two evolving, though we may appear to be one. My soul is hers and it has been since that moment. It will wriggle and writhe and try to burrow closer, deeper, there will be no end. There is no end now. Love presses her magic into all she sees. I am long recovered, I am loverecovered, solid on my legs, solid in the twists, solid in the infernos.

Love may not have created this path or named this path, but she helps me find my way. And I am willing, for the first years of my life. I am certain, for the first years of my life. The screaming is gone and the wars are over, my sweet muse.

I am fearless and swimming in all the luscious things, I am heavy and learning in all the luscious things. I can see, I can hear, I can feel. I don't have to gather and horde. Some things can never be taken, they can never be lost or forgotten. I am standing upon the mountain, bathing in the richness. My hands don't shadowbox anymore, my lips drip sugar. I raise my hands in witness. There is a peace and clarity. There is a rain and a weather in these flames I walk within.

She sets them at my table, she carefully crushes my days with them. She resurrects the man I was supposed to be. She has named me, and I have named her. Love and Leo. We know the insatiable moments, we wear them like ornaments and dreams. Whatever stands outside can stay there and not be seen or heard. I wish it no harm. But I have my Love, my muse, and the clarity. My Love, my muse, and the warm, warm wash, this slow bake into tenderness, these reaching hands and these reaching hearts. In my soul, I know I am home with all the luscious things.

Just knowing we are miles from the fight, miles from the dark and the past. We are miles from that which has doubts for no reason. Put me in your hands, my Love, I am ready to stay home. The compasses have lost their arrows, the maps have lost their roads. There are places to be and places to want. There are places that deserve only to be forgotten. I am not in a place that was earned or deserved. I am in a place that finds me and climbs me, it needs no music or mysteries or stars. I am in a place that holds me, stretches and soothes me, and never confines me. I am simply happy Love has now come home.

Everything may be lingering around, but it does not want us, it is not hungry for us. I believe we are a small piece that keeps the world steady upon its feet. The world needs a little light and redemption to balance the shadows. From what I have learned and what I have heard, the world is an enormous place with corners, with pockets of darkness and listlessness. Love and I aren't the weight or the reason, but I believe our softness is a small piece that helps keep the whole show from hurdling off into the cosmos.

I know I have faith the odds can not always be stacked high. They must fall from time to time, they must whither and fade, find a new place to drink. And they will, long before we will. We can't be pushed through the door, we won't be kept in a box. We desire only what we have. The rest has no place on our backs and shoulders. I know the lovedances blur our vision until we see only the finest things, until we hear only what speaks to us. Let us be free to be gentle. I know I can't find another reason, I know I can't find another desire.

Now that we are lovesoaked we can not be wet, there are no have mores, there are no almosts. I know from my head to my feet and every pulse between. We are loveseasoned and can not be cooked, we can not be eaten. We are lovelost and lovedriven, and we can not be guided. I know the truths that the poisons will not find to weaken, I know what forever feels like. I know it's lightness, I know it's generosity, I know forever speaks without words. There are margins and there are borders and there are restrictions, we can't sense them enough to ignore them.

I know the pain is in the past and it is out there lost in the wilderness. I know there are hands out there with no will and strength, there are faces out there that don't deserve our memory. There are some who don't possess the privilege to be but a ghost. We will not be haunted. I know I can feel the blunt unforgiving time I spent without Love today, and I know she takes it away with her eyes. I know devotion screams no demands, it has no clutches, it is light and easy. I know fascination is a pie I will not eat, not even with cream.

I know history favors the dead, the long long future favors the unborn. I know these years we have chosen to capture us will never be long enough. The passion will never burn enough. I know we are magic, I know we are comfort. I have already forgotten the math and the reality and the reason. I don't want to know what makes sense to the educated mind. The heart knows what it knows, it never forgets, and the rest is treason. The soul knows what it knows, and the rest finds its way into the garbage. Love holds me in her arms again and tomorrow will always be there.

I know the world one day will fall into splinters, but Love and I may never realize it. Some things are difficult and unheard beyond the dream. The fat may be bursting and the starving will be fed. And we may never realize it. I don't want to be released from our bed, I want to walk upon the legs her kisses give me. I want the sweet and the light and the hushes and the promises. I want the world as it allowed us to create it, I want to see where our hands have been. I want us to misbehave beyond the winds, as we are supposed to. I want the long, breathtaking slide, I want the effortless climb. I want to heal in her touch.

I know this kiss from Love and what it means. I know why her hair clings to me. I know why her soul no longer searches and my soul no longer searches. The machines can grind, the noises can grind. I will take Love and all the luscious things.

There are storms, summer storms, winter storms, dust storms, storms with no eyes, storms with strong arms, storms that surprise and storms that linger. There are storms for me and storms for us. There are passion storms that create bedmates and lovestorms that create soulmates. There are storms that poke the day in the eye and storms that will never escape the night.

This one is screaming, it pierces the very guts of the night. It is going to push everything back to its cradle, it is going to take everything right to the edge. My eyes open and I can't tell if it is 3 o'clock or 5 o'clock. 'Did you hear that?' Love says. There is violent driving rain against the window, and terrifying screaming. We are beginning to dress, and the lightning grows angrier. There is no bellowing thunder. There is no sound of wind. This storm has formed naked and true, no clothes, no blankets, no masks. Again and again, the lightning, I've one leg in my shorts, it is taunting me, daring me.

'We can't go out in that,' Love says. The wrenching screams and the windless howling rains threaten to cave the side of the house. The lightning flashes purple, there is still no thunder, but there is drumming, eerie drumming. The screaming stops outside, but it is still in our ears. Love and I are both on the sides of the bed, still half dressed, still certain and uncertain. The final silent eruption was red, I thought I saw a face in it, in the window. There is no more lightning, no drumming, and the rain is only weeping.

Love and I finally finish dressing, she follows me closely, we ease outside. I feel we are walking into a massacre, and I don't know where the monsters are lurking. The air is draped in a darkness, there is a silence we are pushing through. We come around the corner, there is not a leaf or a petal on the ground, not a branch misplaced. The grass is barely damp. Love uses a light to account for all the muses, they are still, if not sleeping, shocked, if not sleeping. I think I see carnage splashed across our window, it is a shadow that flees the light as we approach.

I believe I know what has happened here, but I can't pretend to understand it. Not because of the late hour, not because of the sudden explosion and sudden retreat. It feels like practice for a slaughter, practice for chaos and injustice.

The sky is perfectly clear overhead. It groans, and I know, no one and nothing will admit they saw something tonight. Love is satisfied, but she is not, she is trembling. The muses are resting in the flowerpots, they are resting in the roses. I can throw my shoulders until they are broad, I can walk steadily and purposefully. I can hold Love's hand and we will make our way back inside. But I can't pretend not to know what made those awful sounds and alarming screams tonight.

We will lay quiet and unsettled and hoping for a quiet in our bed for a couple more hours. But this night will not fade and fall from us. We will each hold it in our own way and we will meet in the morning. I have the taste of iron and chains at the back of my throat, I have the taste of the burned and the bothered. Love has the back of her hand across her forehead and tries to close her eyes. Let's rest until we can be out in the daylight, let's rest because the Morning is creeping so close. Let's rest until the Night pulls back its legs.

I know there isn't enough time left to dream and not enough time to wonder. I hope tomorrow, when it finally comes, has no teeth. There will be obligations, but perhaps no teeth. I know much of the world already calls it today. Today will spring from its seed when our steps are ready. We will test our minds and see its slow offerings. I know it will come in tatters, I know it will come in an unspoken boil. I know it will come dressed, I hope it has no horns or hooves.

The day already struggles to keep its shoulders square, it can barely keep its head from dragging across the ground. It is too late to start over, days receive no retakes.

They come, they flow, they stumble, and eventually they pass. Love is convincing herself the muses are fine, now that she can see them in the light. I am convincing myself this is a day to go to work. There is nothing terribly amiss or awfully out of place. I try another cup of coffee. I can't place my finger on it, I struggle to name it. There is love debris, there is soul debris, there is a mess we did not make.

There will be no adventure today, there is nothing demanding, there is nothing calling. The meats are voiceless, they know nothing of time or needs or wants. I will be there as scheduled, I will be paid by the hours, and I will pay with my hands. And Love and her brooms, Love and her shoulders, they will earn it through and through. For the rewards of lights, and air conditioning, food and an old pickup truck, for our house and gardens. And all the nonsense that drags like years behind us. If there were a day to stay home, it feels like today. If that were an option, if that were a question. This is the burn of a sleep interrupted, a dream interrupted. Today is a scorch which is not its own fault.

Some of the trees in the distance, the not so far distance, almost seem new, as though they have been hung there. They are hovering out there like victims. The flies seem off balance and hardly annoying. The bees have a hangover and the hummingbirds can't choose the color of their breakfast. 'The muses seem fine,' Love says. But I am tired, and she is tired. We both need to go out into the world soon, and it would be nice to feel a bit of trust towards it.

But we are gaining our strength and resilience and finding our shoes. The call is growing louder and Love and I will always answer, until we find our quiet, quiet dreams. She is my beauty and my why and my because today, despite our night, and she will be no matter the fits and fists and twists we are given. Surprises fade as quickly as they arise, tiredness can show itself out the door. There is but one mood between Love and I, a mood which sits heavy and constant, a lovemood that remains as the rest flash and float away, a lovemood that passes between our eyes and brings our smiles to our fingertips.

Five years into this chance and this dance and this trance and we can not find a hint of darkness. Five years into the promise and I ache when I hear her say 'My Leo.' Five years into the fray, into the hurricanes, into the blizzards, five years into the challenges that offer nothing more than empty anger and anguish. Five years, I have long learned to fly, I am aware of the man I am. I take Love by her left hand, I take Love by her right hand. I stand firmly beside her and lovingly before her. We can taste the lovepause before we share this kiss we need. This day can be as awkward and clumsy as it chooses to be. Our world is right, it is fantastic. Some words are the truth, whether they are spoken or simply laid upon the dirt. Some words are felt and never heard.

We were patient for 500 years and now we can be eager for 500 years. There is nothing else I can say or do, there is no one else I can be. I can endure whatever this day chooses to become. What we have here is alive and alluring, it is steady and wise, it has its arms out for us. I will see you on the other side of these hills, my love, I will see you on the other side of these waters. And we will find we never left where we needed to be.

This day will be served, the meat will be cut and weighed and priced and sold, and the floors will shine and the countertops will sing. We will not have too far to lean or too far to look for the comfort and the trust. If our backs don't carry our legs, our legs will carry our backs. We know where it feels like home. The hours that may try to dig into us and claw into us, those are the hours Work grips in his hands. When the hunger and the heartaches are over, we can race each other to return here. And I hope this loving madness is spread farther across the world, farther than I know. I hope the juices seep. I hope the way our quiet times saturate us, I hope that is a feeling the whole world knows. I hope the way our satisfaction is just heavy and clings, I hope it stinks, I hope it is sickening, I hope it fills the homes and the yards and the ditches all around the world.

I know there is a place for Love and I and everyone else. Our place is here and then and now. Our place is evolving, endlessly evolving. There comes a time you unconsciously release it all, the darkness and the pain go away, the sadness and the worry lose their weight. I know there is a place. It is in the moment I just experienced and in the moment I am no longer aching for. I do not wait, I dig, I adore, I embellish, I soar. I have given my heart two choices. I can be lovecrushed in this beautiful ambush or never starve.

We are but two in the pull, two in the push. We are a small part of what keeps the world round and the universe challenged. Love searches her way back to me, I claw my way back to her.

There is enough tragedy in the world, there are enough opinions in the world. There are enough ladders in the world and I don't have to climb them. There are enough loveletters in the world and I only have to write hers. I feel as though my hands and knees are done and I am waiting for Love. My empty hours are never truly empty, they are never dangerous, they are never unreasonable. They are laying on the floor like rights, they squeal in their sleep.

And now Trust comes into the light, with her icy blue, stoic gorgeous face. I can sit with her for hours and barely say a word. She knows my head and my dreams, and I come to a quietness. Trust, and all that may fall, trust, and all that may become. There is no sweeter or stronger hand to hold, hers is a voice that searches you. Trust and her depth and her simplicity, trust rushes in rivers the dams will never hold. She is not made of gold or jewels, she does not create fools or kings. She speaks in languages I have heard. I rise for a drink, Love will come home at ten after ten. Trust raises her feet and places them on one of our small tables. 'Like this?' she asks. Yes, like that.

She says she is going to stay a little longer, she likes it here. There are no walls to break and no footholds to create. She likes the words Love and I speak. And then Trust playfully gets into my ribs with her fists, she jokes she is considering spilling out into the night and shouting into the night, telling everyone where we are. I would rather she keep her feet raised and her memory to herself. Trust can share a roof and a roost here, she can have a plate on the table. She finds she has no worries here. She can have her eyes and her talk here, she can bring whatever she wishes.

Car lights spill across the front lawn, and I know what time it is and who is here. I have already dropped my long day, there, outside. Love steps around it as she drops her own. I have eaten and she has eaten, so there is nothing more to do than allow our tables and chairs to bring their legs beneath us.

I know we each are happy to allow the rest of the evening to pass without a ripple. Trust says goodnight, she wanders off, perhaps thinking the hour is not too late to answer some questions somewhere. We breathe through moments that are meant simply to be space holders. There are no distinguishable bridges between the last and the next. There is no reason for the pauses to have any faces.

This is Love and I, and all the rest of the village, and all the rest of the world. Relaxing, knowing we can be nameless and voiceless, spinning in the drift. We can leave it all in boxes and tied up in bags for now, we can see about it all tomorrow. This is nowhere near defeat or submission. This is the unchallenging quiet. The fabric of what we are must contain pieces with no obvious purpose or movement.

We take to our room at a relatively early hour. We don't have long to wait before sleep stops its spinning and begins a slow soft descent. Everything becomes captured in the webs, everything belongs to the hush, everything gets dragged deeper into the hush. I know there is not an inch left for dreams, I know there is no air left for dreams. I know there is no light remaining for all else that could have been done.

TWISTING

We awake leisurely, I eventually make my way to the door. And there it is. Life, dripping wetness, a constant witness. It lays and rolls in the dirt, it floats in the air. It advances through the sludge as easily as it advances through the sweetness. It shows itself like a painting of what you wished for and what you are creating. It holds itself like a mirror so you can see if you have two faces. Life in the clouds, life in the winds and the wings, life at the windows. Life in this passive morning. It will be here whether or not you have the shoulders or the knuckles for it. Love passes by with a hand soft across my back. We are fine.

We've each but one face, worn the same in the light as in the dark. And life knows this. We don't try to challenge or struggle within its flow, we are given this ride, we are taking this ride. The reward is within the delights, within the tones of their songs and the shades of their touches. We don't attempt to lift what we can not grasp. We are comfortably surrounded, and appreciative of the surprises.

Life will rise up to your neck, and then wait for you to learn. It wants you to paddle, it wants you to float, it wants you to feel the currents and not fear them. Life is the swim. It wants to bring you home. I don't yet have the words or the wisdom to describe the forces that create the pain and the cruelty we must all someday experience. But I do not believe life is responsible. There are sinister intentions with sinister hands in the universe.

Perhaps life has come to play today, and watch, and dance. And push and shove. Love and I are too small to resist. Our private corner will flourish, it is too pleasant. Our comforting morning rituals woke themselves, dressed themselves, and carry on by themselves. These are some of the enchantments of the luscious things. This is a day we are allowed to choose the speed and the depth and the motion. Such days do not hide, they want to be found. They want to be loose and curious, they want to be more satisfying than remembered. They are a wave in the swim.

'There is something wrong with the muses,' Love says. Abruptly, things are tidy until they are not. The muses are here but they are listless, some are limp and almost fading. The view and the feel change, as though there is a color missing, a touch missing. I can't name it but I can sense it. There isn't an unsettling crashing sound, it is more of a subtle unraveling whisper. Something is pulling the threads. Our beauties, our roses, our ladies, were proud only yesterday. Now it seems even the most wicked of their thorns have been defied. They seem to bow, they seem to be fearful. They have forgotten their joy.

Instead of a day rich and leisurely, it is to be a day thick with healing. There will be effort and fatigue, we will feel the sun today. Love tries different songs, searching for the one they all seem to hear. I am making wooden stakes and driving them into the soil, if the roses don't remember how to stand I will try to gently teach them. I am being bitten by some, as though they don't want to stand proud again. It is rare to be bitten, when we are saying such nice things to them and calling them beautiful. I am being treated like they don't know me. Gardening never feels like a battle to us, but the wetness seems to no longer want its wet, and the sun seems to want to give us its heat. It is not misery, but it clings like something that is not pleasure.

The afternoon is oily, it is dragging through the tree branches, it is being clumsy on purpose, falling on purpose. We search for a cool spot and a rest. We have done all we can do today. It is time to wait, and rely upon Love's healing hands. It is a long wide stretch between today and tomorrow, until we see what has happened after it becomes dark. I could stand for less of this oil and another cold drink. There is nothing to celebrate, nothing to anticipate. I am still troubled by our quiet spaces being altered. It feels like trespassing, light night stalking. A dreamed enemy, a sleeping threat.

I work a soft kiss onto Love's forehead and she squeezes my fingers. We don't press ourselves out beyond our little paradise, we enjoy the peace within the imaginary

their aim is true and are the only thing in the world that never misses. They are never rushed, they come in a slow melt. The Fever marks the days off the ridiculous calendars because the days have already been cooked and eaten. She tells us we are her babies and she doesn't want us to count the days. The days of Love and I are endless, and we can listen to her, she says, 'Because Time doesn't dress like this, does she?'

The Fever is a welcomed explosion, she has a weight and a longing fury, she has the muscles. She leaves us haggard and happy and hungry. We find ourselves dancing, the closeness in the night shrinks until I can't tell the difference between my arms and Love's arms. She feeds us because she says she doesn't want to find us hungry in a thousand years. Sometimes forever needs a little snack. We love the way the Fever talks. She talks with lips that ache to give. The Fever erupts and never leaves. She never takes the back seat, she never sleeps with the almosts. Love and I gave her our hearts and souls lifetimes ago. She is a wisdom freed from reason, she is a fire freed from touch. She is as endless as the promises she offers, she is more wild than the truth.

The Fever is just what we needed to lay upon the back of this difficult day. Love is fresh and I am mended. We can take a couple more steps into forever. We might not even feel when everything finally collapses into complete nightfall. All the feelings and sensations that grip the world can stay outside. I'll just lose myself a little more, this is the way we are found.

The creatures are out. And we are in. The world may still be talking and chattering, but we are in. It may not be total blindness and deafness but it is deliciously close. It's just the two of us for all the reasons we know, and everything else we haven't learned to hope for.

The Nightmoves are in our room but he appears to be in a mood, I sense he has another place he would rather be. He is distracted, his fine fine shoes betray the steps he is trying to make slide. Something is choking his voice and his rhythm. His songs are struggling, I sense none of his cream and none of his ways. His eyes are darting about tonight, it seems more like worry than mischief. I've never known the Nightmoves to suffer a mood. My hands stop trying to dance and motion to him that everything will be all right. We've got these walls and everything within them. We've got this task of the night. I am not as smooth or pretty as he is, but Love can help me along.

The Nightmoves has his shoes near the door and his hat in his hand, I am waiving aside his apologies. I am struck by the sensation there is something coming and coming fast. It is coming like all we have forgotten and coming like all we can't control. I kiss Love's cheek, I brush her hair aside as though it would be so easy to brush my own thoughts aside. All roads lead somewhere until they cease to be. Our unique road followed us and found us. Some roads lead to ruin, some roads lead to bliss, I can't dismiss all the other roads are bending and breaking into the twist.

We awake to the vulgarity and profanity of a silence we have never heard before. A silence with a chill and teeth, it is an absolute silence, it staggers the senses, it should never walk through such small spaces in the world. I am reaching for doorframes and familiar walls trying to steady myself, my feet are struggling to find the floor. It is a silence that has blackened the windows, the daylight is screaming and being pulled away, it can't reach us, we can't reach it. Love and I are pulling each other through our home. It is a silence that must be escaped, it can't be broken, it can't be fought, it can't be unheard.

I fear it is crushing the roof down upon us. I've barely the strength to open the doors, I am trying to get her out, I am trying to get us out. We fall into a world washed in gray. A grainy, gritty painful world. The silence devours the air and it is so difficult to breathe. This is the silence the stories and the childhood nightmares never spoke about, it is the one that hunts you and craves you, digging deeper and deeper into your ears.

Love and I have never staggered so. We can't find our faces to see. I have never looked around our home and felt this. The silence reeks, it burns the nose and eyes, it has become so confident it turns a deep saddening blue, it has grown arms and legs. It lunges at us, it threatens us, it has a horrific bark. The angry, belligerent silence, it was left on the pot to boil and it was forgotten. And now we must walk through it. We never asked for it, it festered and rotted and grew a purpose and a focus, it is up in a stance now and acting vengeful.

The sweet gentle quiet can not be found, the peace outside the noise can not be found. We have only this grotesque silence, threatening to crush everyone and everything. I don't understand why it came to our little paradise, why it came to this harmonious place. Love grabs my arm and says, 'Oh, Leo.'

And I finally see everything is gone.

It, they, what, came for the simple, for the subtle, for what could be reached. Our beautiful, imperfect corner of this world, the one that is now devastated. It has been ravaged and ruined beyond what even memory can repair and return. What was wanted, what was lovingly created. The fires don't even burn now, the ashes are being scattered in the breeze. The love, the colors, the blooms, the mysteries. They haven't been stolen, they haven't disappeared. It is wrenching, they were taken, taken from the earth, taken from a small breath of history, taken from us. As though they never existed. It was a target, as opposed to power, it was a target, as opposed to wealth. When the subtle and pleasant is lost, the loud and obvious loses its grasp and footing. The silence is now so deep and proud, it wants to allow anguish and tears. The silence has been starving for a moment like this.

There is nothing to collect, there is nothing to recover, even that which was rooted deepest did not survive. This is the picture of when brutality decides it will suffer kindness no more. There is nothing but loss, inexplicable loss. The tenderness and the beauty, we slept through their massacre. The peace and the promises, we slept through theirs, too. There was pleasure and magic here, a feast of the luscious life. We did not abandon it, we did not stop believing, we never stopped reaching or evolving.

There were fabulous pieces, moments of our hearts and souls, and all the muses, and all the flowers. Vanished. Taken. All that remains are shreds of terror and chaos. And everything that was not meant to be is drifting in the grass. A pure fury and anger and resentment is building, they have no place here. But they are in my eyes, in my hands. I am remembering them now. The silence is losing its courage, suddenly, and retreating towards the trees. There should be consequences when savagery takes beauty from this world. There should be a revolution when the silence tries to steal the words.

I find the twist is deep and wretched within me.

I am supposed to walk through all the hours and all the obligations today. I am supposed to dress for today. But all I can see is the expression on Love's face and the ghost in front of it. 'I will find the pieces,' she says. I worry over her giving heart, and I see nothing she can resurrect and everything she can try. But then, I have never doubted her, I have never clawed her or questioned her, I have never clouded her. I don't want to leave for the day and I don't want Love's feet in the muck. She tells me she will find the pieces and make them whole. She is telling my head not to worry.

If there was a day I trust her most, it is today. Today is a burden, it is a coat I can not wear.

Love leaves me at the front door in my clothes, with a lunch, an embrace, a kiss and a promise. I will come back to risk it all and dare it all, and Love says she will break this day and be waiting for me tonight. I get another kiss and some new legs and I am kicking this day as though it has kicked me. And telling the hours they will lay down in front of me.

I will feel what trickles down my arms, I will see what is my real dreams. She is the one I ached for, the one I waited for, and I am choked into all the luscious things. I want to dance the way she wants me to dance with her. I want that freedom through the fall. I know what it is and will never loosen my grip. I know of no other way to breathe. I want to come home and show Love what we have in our hands. She will kiss me once and tell me she remembers, she will kiss me a second time and tell me she knows. And I will believe her, I will believe her more than anything this day may try to teach.

The twist will be when all the angels are upon your back and they invite all the devils. I feel like I know this night like I know the rain on my face. I know I am home, I know where we go and where we will never be. The twist tries to squirm and find its way between our clasping fingers, it can not find room between our eyes, it can not find room between our teeth, it will never make us forget. It can not come between our loving blows.

I stumble into this aching want, it is just beyond the lights, it is just beyond everything I have missed. And there is nothing wrong. Love comes from our room, she has the look of the devastated, she has the look of one who has heard the truth and she has it on her shoulders, she has no choice but to try to lay down with it. Her hair is a mess and she is absolutely beautiful.

I am home again and Love walks in like she is my chance to forget everything I have ever seen and ever known. She walks with hips that have taught me everything I want to be. She loosens her smile and untucks her shirt and grabs me by the hands. She loves the man I promised to be, and I promise her before she asks again.

Love needs only one thing, and I promise her in the light and the dark before she speaks. Anything in the world, anything in the depths, anything in the flavors we plow and the flavors we know, anything we keep or need or have. There is only one muse remaining, it is lost but not abandoned. There is but one muse left, it is resting in a glass of water beneath a single flower on the windowsill in our kitchen. It is safe, it huddles, it is rescued and it is frightened. Nothing else is left.

Love tells me to take a moment, I refuse, but then I do. The remains of the day are fading, their coolness offers no comfort, their warmth offers no comfort. The devastation and the rubble have been swept away. What we discovered this morning is hidden, but not gone. The empty angry spaces speak of it. The beautiful is now the barren, and my heart is sick with it. I don't know what Love has suffered but she is pale with it.

She tells me she needs my shoulders and my back. This one last little muse speaks to her when she sings to it. Love needs my will, and she tells me so. I stand outside and my eyes refuse to believe what they see. Our hands began to shape all of this, our hands startled the soil and stirred the growth and shared the hours and opened our eyes. And something took it. It took the subtle and the sublime, it took the enchantment, the provocative, it stole the sense and the scents.

In this heavy, heavy light I can remember all that was and all I can not see. The violence redressed what we knew and what we shared. I follow her inside. My Love is fading, she is sinking and weakening, and each time I offer myself, she raises her hand as though she is not the one to be saved. She is in the air, she hasn't been harmed, but she hasn't the strength for the twisting swim. My Love is drifting from pink to pale, and it is tearing apart my insides, slowly, piece by aching piece. There has never been a monster to come between us, there has never been a nightmare to come between us. I see clearly. It is all in shambles, the darkness is coming, it is surrounding us, it is pressing its steps all around us.

Love's smile and face seem to have been eaten by the hours. The minutes and the seconds are crawling all over her. She leaves her hands in mine. I expect a burst. I am waiting for her colors to explode again. I receive a twinkle and a promise. I receive a tickle and a hint. Love speaks to me with her soul, her ravishing soul, her deep throated soul. Her exquisite, gentle soul. In a voice I will never forget.

'Leo, I need you to find them.'

The roses are gone, the flowerpots are gone, all the gorgeous and the garnishments are gone. The truths and the knowns are hanging by the threads and hanging in the vines, the depths seem to have lost their place and have been replaced by the angry lurking shallows. Love seems to fade with every kiss, but she says no, no, she needs me tonight. Her eyes are wet and her hunger is losing ground to the tired. I am beginning to understand, she needs only what I have always promised her. I will take the weight on my back, the darkness in my face, and our sun in my memory. I will take it with my hands, my legs, my shoulders, I will take it in the teeth. I will take it across my brow, I will take it in the guts. She has nothing more to give tonight, so I will take my kiss as the happiest man alive. I have a promise I must keep.

Love does not bring me a challenge, she brings the last sweet muse. They can both do no more, they can offer no more, they can suffer no more. The muse points to the darkest place I have yet to be tonight. The known is behind me, the unknown is slamming the doors. The answer is hidden somewhere before me. The drowning and the churning are coming.

Find them. The paste and the hesitation are leaving, the old hands and their old determination are coming, the slick and the unwanted, the lost and the needed, the had and the unforgotten, they are all out there. Just in the dark. Just past the spit, being gripped in the spirit.

'Please find them,' Love says. I know she speaks of the muses and nothing else, for everything else can be replanted and regrown. Love and the last little muse are exhausted, their minds and their hearts need not a cure but a recovery. Everything is gone, the singing and the pleasure, the beauty, even the ugliness. I am somewhere between what we have known and what we have lost. Somewhere between the luscious choices and the consequences. I feel there is no need to ask forgiveness, none will be offered.

We lovingly carved a subtle, sublime place in this world. We created no harm, we created no reason to harm. It won't be forgotten, it won't be dismissed as something not meant to be. Love has surrendered beneath the covers, she has no legs remaining, no strength remaining. I want to give her peace. I will accept the burden. She has no fight remaining. She can't open her eyes to my last kiss, she responds barely with a breath to my last touch.

I have never known Love to be crushed. I will call it sleep and not defeat, tiredness and not agony. There are some words we do not speak in our language. I am outside, I see in the window the last muse appears safe. Again, it points to the darkest place, and then twists from sight, hiding beneath one last flower.

LABORING

I am in the darkness that has pooled, in the icy biting shards that have pooled. The shadows will not lay here. The Night will not bring its feet here. I have no plan, I have no ideas, I have no compass or map or friends out here. And when you are friendless in the pool you know it. You feel it. It wraps around your bones, and then your eyes and your ears, and your legs and guts are left in charge. I can feel a slight rage in my fingertips, and a sense of injustice.

I find myself as calm as a statue. The night noises are all about, they are somewhere else, they are meant for someone else. There is nowhere to go, there is nothing to find. I have this paralyzing calmness about me. I am waiting to be found, I am waiting to be told. I am defiantly silent, defiantly still. Whether it is a road or a path, it is nothing to be discovered, it is nothing that has been made or prepared. The darkness is waiting in ambush, it is deciding whether I am the face it is looking for. I know nothing but am aware enough I do not have to seek. I have come here to be found. I am being hunted, I am being lured.

I am in the pool, in the darkness, because that is what I told Love I would do. I await the mouth. I don't know its hunger and I can not imagine its thirst, but I am in the pool. I am here with flesh and bones. I am not the spectacle or the hero, I am the slaughter, I am the feast.

I don't believe I can get out, even should I try. And the dim lights from our home that were seemingly just behind me are now farther away. In my mind I hear 'Go find them.' In my heart I hear new and strange terrible grumblings, stomach panic and stomach longings. I am here in the pool with little more than a shirt and shoes, I am not equipped as an adventurer or a fighter. I am the willing. I can not remember if the muse said these will be labors or trials. I see my home is farther away than it was before. If the pool was not so cold, I might consider it stale and stagnant, but it has some motion beneath its silence, it brings some fear with its mystery.

I am not reaching out into this darkness, it is pulling me in, steadily, forcefully. There is some belief beyond the defiance, and now I hear sickening laughter. There are secrets, heavy, heavy, in their place. There are rules never spoken or written, there are rules that change in spinning hands. There are things even the darkness can not abide. But there are gifts, and memories, and promises made and promises unbroken. So as the pool twists into a drift, I remember I am but a man, but I am her man. I feel so very alone and my home is fading and fading. The teeth and the deep are pressing ever closer. I hope Love is fast asleep in our bed and the last muse is safe in our window. The gnawing laughter comes from where I can not see.

The path is taking me, there is no lead or follow. It is closer to aggression. There is no need to even pretend I know where I am going or that I will understand what I am supposed to do, when the time comes, should the time come. The lingering dread changes to panic with a sudden bite. The panic is too reckless and childish for me to believe it is the source of any of this. There is a breathing growing louder, the choking vines are hanging thicker, there are turns to nowhere and nothing. Something is trying to show me its will is greater than mine. The panic has been replaced by Fear, or perhaps it has been Fear all along.

Fear in its most pure and free form. Out in its jungle, out in its playground. Fear with its tongue against your edges, fear with its tongue against your judgement and experience. One will conquer and one will cry. I turn around, and see there is nothing behind me, there is nothing to return to, there is no escape. There is but the push forward. Fear brings out the noises and they are growing more brave and they are coming closer. Out here the noises can not be named or recognized, they can't be rationalized, the noises pursue, they can be fierce, they can be maddening, they can make you question whether you heard them at all. They will not be dismissed. Fear can not be bargained with, it wants to be pleaded with, it wants your face at its knees, it wants your hands clutching its pants, it wants your mouth warm and wet with sobs and confusion.

I am moving deeper, if I am moving at all. I feel I am falling, I feel I am already failing. This must be Fear's home and creation, unseen by the other elements. It is unfiltered and beyond their influence. Fear knocks the noises around with its fists. There are no lights to muffle it, no doors to close and hide it. There is no comfort, no reassurance, there is no shield, no veil. Fear wears the crown, Fear sits upon the throne.

There are roaming howling noises running in packs all around, they are hunting as tribes, swirling like winds. I hear them like the eyes of snakes lying in wait in the tall grasses, I hear them like the jaws of spiders racing down their webs from the trees. Fear wants to crush me with its company, it wants to see if I will run blindly into the darkness, away from the noises, away from the onslaught, into its stomach. It is rippling through me, it wants to hear the sound of my knees falling to the ground. It is chattering to me, it is whispering to me, it explodes like thunder. It is waiting for that first delicious moment when I should close my eyes in surrender and cover my ears. That is when I would be so succulent and tender.

Fear works its everchanging grip, it is looking for the triggers, it is searching and probing for the triggers. There is no pause out here, there is no relief, no refuge. There is only Fear and I, and I am surrounded and outnumbered. It wants just a tasty bite, maybe just at my ribs, maybe at the back of my neck. There are flies landing to try to soften me up. The noises have eased until I find myself wondering where they are. They are not at my heels, they are not flicking at my ears. Fear throws three bursting laughs at me into the jungle. One for what I thought I knew, one for what I believed, and one for me.

If Fear can't make me crawl, perhaps it can make me climb, if it can't make me sing it might make me speak. I shake but I do not quiver, I shuffle but I do not stumble. I feel a storm coming, a new storm, and it stinks like rage. My throat is so dry, and I can't feel what I have and what I have lost. The explosions are building, they are marching in from the distance, they are forming lines and finding their way. Softness finds my ear, softness has somehow found its way, it sounds so pleasant and easy, speaking to me in a strange voice. 'There, there, Leo, just give it what it wants.' And then it buzzes like an insect and flinches like a trick. Softness has the smell of someone else's friend. Fear is waiting. Fear is hungry, and it always gets what it chases.

Fear promises numbness and very few memories after it consumes you. I see its teeth in a mouth that never whispered and kept a promise, not as I did. I see its teeth in a mouth that never tasted the truth, not as I did. A storm is coming and everything seems to be a little quieter. It feels as though the hands have lightened from my shoulders. Fear remains, it wants the soak, it wants the bath, it wants the feast. The darkness has not completely released my legs, but it no longer spins me by my hips.

Fear has taken away all the questions, it has pulled me away from my own steps. It is not subtle, it wants to possess, and it wants it gifted. It waits as though it has exhausted all its deception. That which were waves are now slow drips, that which was savage can now barely be heard. A storm is coming but I do not feel the pursuit. Softness has long arms and strong hands and a stained face I do not seem to recognize. I believe I see a glimpse, a tail of a light I hope was meant for me. I feel a hint of a first lovekiss, as Fear squeezes me, for the first time or the last.

A storm is coming but it is loose and has lost its filth. It is not a storm I can escape, it is not a storm that was meant for me. There is a light within the madness, it lays in the darkness between this and the next. A trench in time fashioned with loveshovels. I feel a moment of home and I feel I have never been further away. I feel a moment of home and I must endure what awaits.

Fear is gone. It is not bested or defeated, it is no longer mine. We may know each other again, because forever and always is a long time. I can almost envision my Love sleeping, I am far from her hands and she is beyond my reach.

There is a wisdom beyond what we freely know and freely speak of, it remains hidden inside us, if we are fortunate. I am unlucky, I am within a sliver of the universe never intended for humanity. The true Elements have abandoned this place, they do not come to play in the wreckage. Even those Elements that have surrendered their hearts still have memories. The rest have souls. I have come to the place where the bones of Courage rest. The bones are dusty and they have aged, they sit upon a bench with one leg thrown across the other. As though it was waiting for someone or something, or was simply satisfied with itself. Courage had a whistle in its pocket and a bone in another, it may have wanted to tell us something.

This is where Fear abandoned its empathy, this is where it became swollen. This is where Fear chose to forget who it was. This is where Fear chose to walk among us and not with us, this is where Fear chose to speak to us and not teach us.

I haven't the room or the guile or the smile for another challenge. But then, in this quiet quiet moment, I feel her lovetouch, she is blindly tossing lovehands in her sleep. They are finding their way and they are finding me, like a pretty pretty shower. It is too much to carry, it is too much for pails, it is too much for tankers. My legs are more of a drifter than a traveler. I drifted home before I understood, I drifted into the nets, I drifted into the dreams, I was too deep before I realized what I discovered.

This calm feels fleeting at best and there is movement, steady movement, all around and above and beneath and in between. There is a feeling that weighs like a voice. We may not have been the targets or the victims but perhaps a sweet captured taste within the chaos. The sirens found their numbers and their perfect place. And here I am in the drift, and the hours and the miles can not be counted, being so far from where I need to be.

These are places I am now discovering, hidden places that should not be found. Every corner has a voice, every turn has a hand, every climb has push. I don't want Love's wings here, they could not breathe. I don't want Love's voice here, its song would be stolen. I am beyond the mentioned and the known and nearing what should never be remembered. I am no hero, I am no brave, I am no soldier. I still feel the promise I carry, the promise I intend to keep.

There seems no purpose here for bones which have life. For bones which have dreams and joy. There is no warmth for kissing souls, there is no warmth to speak of at all.

I feel the heavy drag within the drift. Everything speaks in blue and gray, everything wilts with dismay and moans. A fever can not live here, a candle can not live here. Sadness keeps its thumbs pressed hard upon its dungeons. These are walls I thought I would never see again. This is Sadness, now that it has learned to keep its hand at a throat, now that it believes it can outlast us. And all the while, almost unnoticed, it runs a steady finger back and forth, back and forth, across the heart it wants to claim. Sadness leaks into this mist, and the mist wants only to entangle me, to slow my steps, to hinder me, to make me pause and make me think and make me regret. The mist seeps, it wants me to believe I need it. It wants me to carry it.

Oh, this silent dragging Sadness I have not seen for so many years. It mopes and hopes I wear its clothes and eat its dishes. It lurks and follows, it will follow you steady, until it surprises you, and then it has you. And then it is too late. You can't run from it and you can't swim against it. Sadness assumes all the angels are too occupied to protect us all. It looks for the stray lamb that believes itself to be a fighter. There are chairs at the tables, it is looking for someone to eat. Sadness is not the beast or the banquet or the feast I am looking for. But I am lost with no reason and no direction. I have been the picture of happiness, and now Sadness wants to drag its tongue across the glass and the frame. To taste me one last time. The memories are succumbing to the mood out here, I fight to know where I came from. My hands knew luscious wonders and the Sadness wants to steal them from my fingers like candy.

The Sadness hovers, making no sudden moves and no violence and no penetration. It lounges, it prefers to be accepted, it dribbles, it spills like an accident, and then it clings like an ache that won't be mended. Sadness crawls slowly so you don't realize you are being overcome, it changes like walls, it oozes like wounds to be bound. And then you are bound and unhealed. I try to find the feeling in my hands. Sadness wants to kiss my face, it wants me to feel its thickness and weight. These feel like walls I don't want to remember.

It doesn't move, it waits lazily, it wants to feed, it wants to smother. Sadness craves a slow choke, first it takes half your breaths, and then it wants your permission to breathe again. It doesn't want you to know the chains are there, it leaves them loose, until you barely recognize the tightening. I can barely feel how far I have moved into it, I am just realizing how sloppy and slow my steps have become. I didn't realize it was stealing my footprints. Sadness and its slow strangle does not have to be worked into and does not want to be worked out of. Sadness and all that droops and suffers quietly. Everything seems so impossible once its yolk is around your neck.

I am aching for a familiar voice, I am aching for a voice of treason and escape. Sadness is relentless and pressing, it has a hollowness that threatens to carve me, it has a girth that threatens to crush me. It is creating these long narrowing halls before I reach them. I know I must suffer them. Sadness stretches them longer still, it squeezes them closer. I feel the dampness before I touch it. The walls are trying to speak to me in its voice. This is not the chase Fear brought, this is not the hunt. I don't need to look behind me. It is all around me.

Sadness begins to play its slow drums, its hollow painful drums. I convince myself to keep moving, searching for a thought, just a memory of light. Sadness hasn't the strength to hold me, not until I choose to lay down, not until I begin to surrender. Only then can it use its laziness, its weight, its stubbornness and enormity. This passage is growing slim and tight, the ceiling is lowering, the drums are scratching at my back.

I can hear the dragging of its nets, it pulls them along looking for sinking treasures, looking for easy treasures with no fight. Endless woven twisted and gnarled nets, they are filled with old loss and new pain. They have been dragged so carelessly for so long there are no longer any names for the faces inside. There is just the growing bitterness that can not find its way free through the ropes. I have to break free of the grip. I can stay ahead of it, if I just use the left and then the right, the left, the right. I ignore how close it is behind me. I can't ignore that these walls have closed to brush against my shoulders.

116

Sadness wants to be heavy upon the back, heavy in the ears, it wants our hands at our chests like a prayer. It wants no taste in our mouths, no music in our eyes. So we might pause, and then remember, and then worry, and then obsess. It offers a quilt and a blanket. It can be taken like a pill, taken like a bullet. Sadness needs but some room and space, it needs you to be still and quiet, and that is when it becomes the loudest. It will drown you with no noise and no haste. Its wheels and gears will work over you. Sadness tells me it has something in its nets for me, something special, something I might like, if I would only stop and take a look. It asks me why should I hurry into something that is undecided and unpredictable, it has the cold press of what has already been tried and what has already failed. Remembering is much easier than awakening. Missing is effortless. Regretting is effortless. Attempting is frightening.

Sadness is offering its long cold stone path. I am fighting to keep a thought of my own, fighting to keep its voice out of my head. It is moaning and tired behind me. No, no I do not want to take a rest, I do not want to think for a minute. Sadness is brushing at my elbows, it is pulling at the back of my shirt. I have no meat on me. Perhaps a kiss could find the sugar and spice. Perhaps an embrace could relieve some of this burden. I realize I am being pressed into an angry corner, and Sadness is no longer walking right behind my steps, it has surrounded me. It is trying to gnaw at me, take me, even as I am being pressed into the walls, pressed into impossibly small spiderweb cracks.

I am violently pushed free by a river of names and faces and years that no longer have voices. I am pushed by all I no longer hold. I am pushed because what I lost does not have the weight of what I have. I am crushed and forced through. I spill into a tepid bath of memory, I have only a feel of Sadness' teeth on my back. And for a few moments, I wonder if I will stand.

This is not a night or day or a path. This may never be a memory and this should never be a memory. I am where I was never meant to be. I am far from somewhere. I can't reach my home. I feel my face is cracked. This is not the Sirens' work, this is not the Sirens' rage or their plan. This is the aftertaste, this is the aftermath, these are the piles of broken pieces they have left behind.

The Sirens' wails raised rooftops and encircled buildings like smoke. They brought out the doubtful and the curious and slaughtered them all the same, and they sought out the meek and the frightened and made meals of them. Their savage night and destructive morning and days to come. It was all but a whim. Just an instant. They stretched their legs and their wares, their voices and their hands, they cleared their throats. All to escape their tunnels, to fuel their vanity, to admit their sickness.

If this is suffering it must have more of a purpose. I can endure anything if I could have just the next moment with Love. If I could just see her with those eyes, if I could just give her those words. I feel I must stand again. My Love, our depth is our simplicity, our nature is our reward, our hearts will not be ravaged, our souls will not be touched. We can see the colors of our minds and our sensibilities. If she can help me move again, get me through the rust and the ruins. I want to see the truth and beauty again, find the light thundersteps, I will have to endure and forget the journey again. I wonder now if I see a glimpse of her face in the distance. It is enough to make me stand and seek the one I made the promise to.

There is a cloud ahead, and that is undoubtedly where I must go. I do not know how I am going home, there is nothing behind me, there is no trace, no air, no space. I could see more easily through a sheet of black. This is an impossible cloud, a rock of a cloud, a treacherous cloud. It is my only way forward, my only way into the blindness. There is an angry rip in the shape of a smile. I can either go in willingly, or I will be dragged certainly. There is a flame in the distance and the insects are heading that way and the creatures in the night with eyes are heading that way, and so must I.

After two steps I am in the wash, I am in this new spill, I am in the new terrible. I sluggishly fight against it as though I am in a dream. My arms can not tear through anything, my legs are in another state of surrender. The flame is a massive fire and me and the insects and the madness are racing towards it as fast as the cloud is racing from it.

Old Hands plays in the fire, Old Hands feeds it, they are all I can see. I can hear the insects burst as they near it, I can feel the coals as they dance. I am in a blind tumble, and Old Hands are waiting for me. I stop in a sudden heap, they are close around me but not yet touching. They have built this place, they have kept this place, and they dare me to come uninvited. Old Hands flex, maybe to challenge, maybe to fight, maybe to question if I don't remember them. Massive and scarred and gnarled as if by centuries, they change to useless and weak and worthless. They grab the fire by the throat and seek me again and ask if I remember them as they remember me.

Old Hands open, one and then the next, one has harmony inside and the other doubt. They close again quickly, they aren't offering a choice, they aren't asking questions. I have to find my way out of their fingers to even think for a moment. Old Hands open with softness and ridicule. They are searching me now, they are picking and poking and prodding. They are looking for not a language or a dialect, not a dream, no, no they are asking for a barrage I understand, they are asking for a tongue I understand. They wear rings and speak persuasion and become suddenly angry when they see me looking around.

Old Hands are bitter beneath the rage, they have forgotten how to hold, they have forgotten what it is to need. They have been worn and owned by too many to count. The priceless and the poor, the famous and the forgotten, the living and the real. Old Hands wants something for my trespassing. A coin for a coin. A truth for a truth. A betrayal for a betrayal. They have no interest in my pockets, they have no interest in the chases I have escaped. Empty hands do not fool them, the meat is within. They check my shoulders, they check for wings, they count my bones one by one, they look hungrily through my intentions.

And who have they belonged to, everyone and no one. They have held sand and water, fruit and invention, animals and stones, truth and the dirty filthy lies. Old Hands can hold a cough just as they can hold a secret. They can hold a nightmare and a dream and they can hold a cost. They can crush me, but I am delivered from here. They open and close, the Old Hands, one has temptation and the other one has reward. I sit at this fire because I will never succumb to this fire.

Here we are, memory to memory, patience to patience, leg to leg, nail to nail. It shows me its eyes of Betrayal. I am within reach of the fire and feel no flames. Old Hands know how to search, they know how to feel, they know how to color temptation into destruction. If they ask for but a moment, they will take an hour, if they ask for but a day, they will take a lifetime. They tell me I stink of completion and satisfaction, I carry too much that I am not willing to part with. They flip coins at me. Patience for beauty. The coins land at my feet. Truth for pleasure. New for old. The coins strike my legs. Substance for lust. Lustfulness for nothing. Success for value. Riches for sensuality. I am beginning to see their eyes turn yellow. I will remain unbent at this fire.

There are things that have no price, there are things that have no equal. There are some things the Old Hands can not hold, they can not steal. There are luscious things that make you twist and make you smile. There are luscious things that have no doubt and no burden. There is life that can not be touched or burned by betrayal. There is life that grips you so tight and makes you so free. All the pretty voices and all the pretty faces can not sway you. There are feelings the Old Hands can not reach, not matter how well it is disguised. Betrayal is acting as though it is suddenly cold beside its own fire.

I don't seek what I already hold dear, I don't look beyond what I already see. The cloud is unraveling and the fire is dimming. There are pleasures I do not know and do not wish to feel. They await, wet in the swim. I have nothing to offer and nothing to barter. The satisfactions, the fulfillment, the contentment, they are wild and they are ours. They come to me in the light and they return to me in this darkening trap, this harness. I can see Betrayal's real and sickly face now. And I stare back at him with a face of a man who ages, a man who sings, a man who learns and a man who digs. I give him the face of a man who has deep, deep fingers within the luscious things, the face of a man who wants to be home again.

Betrayal's spent coins are on the ground. I will step around them and step over them and not through them. I want to be lifted, I want to be calmed. I want to rescue and be rescued. I want to be ravaged. I freely walk away into a slow crumbling want.

And the Sirens gained nothing from all of this, nothing changed after their feast. Only the gratification from the stolen peace, my peace, our peace. They gave legs to unspoken desires and won and lost nothing. Now there is only the taste of turmoil and the smoldering wreckage. The earth is not scorched, the day will be recovered, and history will not remember. Those who were not taken will not notice the ashes, and those taken will beg and forget.

They have had their fill and wetted their appetites, but they will never walk among the Elements. They have returned to their caves, their moments and conquests wash along with the waters. They have no hold upon us, despite their screams and songs and recklessness. I don't want to know what they have done. I have eyes for such other things. I slept through their rampage. And now I am here, not for the roses, not for the plants or their pots or their plates, not for the destruction or the pleasure or the pain. I am here for a promise.

In this hesitation so brief, I hear the way we speak and walk, I feel the way we talk and love. I feel it beyond our arms and legs, I feel it as we crawl into our eyes, I feel it in our roots, and if I could just taste the longing of one more kiss, if I could hold the moment of one more kiss. If I could fall into one of our memories. I am absolutely alone on a path that was never meant for me. Fear and Sadness and Betrayal are behind me, and I don't want to lose myself to what awaits beyond.

I have not found the muses, I have seen no trace. This is not a path, it is a terror. There are no answers, there are no sounds, there is no way forward and no way back. I am resented and resisted, there is nowhere I belong. The light has no warmth here, the light makes no effort to separate itself from the darkness. The light does not even take shelter. I feel a long hair calling and it lands across my shoulders and collects around my neck. I sit here, for a moment. I'll sit here for a moment as though someone is reaching out to me. Reaching for me, clinging to me, and as things become more beautiful and precious and rare, they are becoming more real, they are becoming as they were. And the blues are deep and rich and the reds are becoming more vibrant and alive and colors are speaking to me as though I am slowly remembering.

Another clings, like a hair, and now another, around my face, around each arm, and now my legs. One down my shirt in delight and one across my lips in a scream. They search between my fingers, and down my pants, and now I know it is too much. There are too many, this is too much. I stand to be dragged, I rise to be taken. I am in the webs. They are sucking and grasping, they are feeding. I can lay down and be torn, or I can struggle and be ripped to unrecognizable pieces. I can let it fill my heart and my mouth.

Doubt is up the hill, and it is using its hooks and pulling on its levers. It can bring me up, slow and crazy and clean, or it can shove down the dirt and the rocks and the hill it wants me to climb. It can feed me to the cactus, or drown me in the water.

Doubt can raise a hand as though it is opening a door. It brings an awful embrace, it whispers to you, your legs aren't ready, your legs can't do it. It brings a terrifying face and wants to kiss your lips. I am being brought up its hill before I can feel anything. There is only the invasiveness, the penetration, and the cold. I am in Doubt's webs and I have to stop twisting before I can find my way free. Doubt is the hand that lingers, it is the dirty mouth at the dinner, it is the beggar that says you can not do more.

Doubt will carry you only so far before it wills you to fail and crumble. It comes like an old toothy friend, and turns into a talkative one. It comes with slow, quiet steps, it comes like a stranger, it looks down its long nose across what you have and all you have done. To the diligent, it is close to suffocation. To the ambitious, it is utter defeat. Doubt will walk across you, cold, it wants to check for crevices, it craves an entrance.

I feel the chill and the anxiety, here on its hill. Even more now that the webs are gone. It speaks methodically when it speaks at all. Doubt is divinely patient, it can outlast anyone, especially when it is playing its own game. It is odorless and tasteless and its grip is contagious, it can work its way through a crowded room. It is never clever or charming, it is steady, brooding and searching. I feel as though I am forced to sit with it, and I am wondering, becoming quietly curious. I wonder how soft I am, I wonder how easily manipulated I am.

My home and all I have known seem not lost or taken, but thrown. I wonder if there will be a path to return. Doubt begins to drip and I barely notice. It won't come in a sudden vicious wave, it won't come with lights or heat or bursts. It nibbles so you don't believe it wants to swallow you and ingest you. Doubt will pretend to be confusion, it wants to place you in the folds, it subtly, carefully directs you down into the caverns. That is where the near darkness lives, that is where the fight becomes submission. That is where the match strikes the melt, that is where certainty becomes cream. The whispers which began quietly now become louder. Doubt's clutches arrive beneath the surface, the clutches close and unseen, they are not felt. It is too late.

The drips continue to come and I pass them off as rain. Doubt's words are spilling like soup, and I am only now realizing I am reaching for a bowl and a spoon, I am only just realizing I am sitting upon its hill as though I belong here. Alone I am easier prey, alone I am attentive prey. This strange and mystical push is all about, it surrounds me. Doubt asks if I would like to lay down, there will be no pain. There is bread in my left hand and a bowl in my right. Perhaps this drift has come to this, perhaps it has become unbearable. The ground feels soft and gentle beneath me. The soup has thickened into a savory stew.

Doubt offers me a comfortless smile. There is only so much a mind can be asked to withstand. There is only so far a soul will travel. There are limits to the human heart. I can almost hear myself asking for the butter. He keeps speaking, assuring there is a cave just for me and a quiet just for me. I don't have wings and neither does she. My legs can give up because this path leads nowhere. There is nothing to find and nothing to expect.

The drips continue, solid, splashing, soaking, it is difficult to wipe them from my hair, my arms. Doubt studies me straight, through and through. It is looking for a collapse, it is waiting. I close my eyes, it tells me the sun will not be there. I sit rigid and raw, it tells me everything will not return. Nothing will be as it was. But I will open my eyes again. I will open my eyes learned and not new. I fail to open them in this moment, I will open them in the next. I know only one truth. And she returns to me in this awful twist.

I can't find Love's face in this madness. But I somehow trust there is room for purity in this world, even within this strange part I am trapped in. Doubt pretends to aimlessly shuffle through its weights. It pretends to accidentally kick the mud. It has some blankets, just over there, it offers. I watch it running its fingers across its treasures of waits and almosts and can'ts. I haven't eaten a single mouthful, I haven't taken a bite, I haven't tested the gravy to see whether it is cooled or boiling. I feel as though I am fighting off a mask, squirming from the shackles. I haven't felt what I remember I long to feel, I haven't felt what I have always known.

For all the sleepy sickness it causes, Doubt's impatience is beginning to show through its skin, its impatience is a spice upon its breath, a stumble in its words. Its hands are not the heaviest I have felt tonight. Doubt seems to wish to quarrel, but it is too lazy to do so. I am drying and my legs feel the urge to stretch. It offers me a blanket for the cold I do not feel. I have an uneaten stew in my hand and am remembering myself. It offers a problem to fight the courage and a failure to find the night, a sheet to cover the faces and a pillow to cover the voices.

Love comes into my mind, she is raw and beautiful, and for a moment I am no longer alone. There must be a reason for this path. Perhaps it is to endure, perhaps it is not to forget. Doubt screams suddenly as though it were struck. And then sits on its haunches and asks why I want to leave. I understand it can not just possess me, it can not influence the unwilling. Doubt will have to wait for another.

There is a sliver of light, just over there, it could be mistaken for a sunrise, and perhaps I can begin to hope I will make it through this night. Even the longest paths carried by impossible nights must have an end. I have to believe.

Somewhere beyond what I am struggling to endure, I believe the world is no longer suffering, it is regathering in the dawn. It is counting and collecting the pieces, the dust is being swept back into the corners. The rampage is over and the Sirens will go back into hiding, their allure is fading, their voices are fading. They will once again be found only by the fools who seek them. The Sirens will once again be lost to all but those who are curious about their charms. I sense the scattered Elements are circling and rediscovering and assuming their places.

I still have a promise to fulfill, but I don't believe it will be done in this swamp and this filth I have entered. I focus upon following my own steps, avoiding the wet fingers that are searching in horrible trickles. This is an unkept filth beyond reason, an unnatural filth with spying eyes. The smell is obnoxious and choking but it can't be endless. I have learned this night that nothing can be endless. I have learned this night that everything can be suffered and endured. This filth festers and writhes in its own insignificant place and time. It fails to reach beyond. Its pulse and flavor are nothing more than disgust, and disgust exists in a shrinking world. This swamp has no pull or purpose, it has no persuasion. I can see its end just through the trees ahead, and these legs are finding their strength, my eyes are finding the light.

I promised Love I would find the muses, and now I sense the slow lingering ache of belief, an ache I nearly feared I had lost. This was meant to seem impossible, but it was not forever. These labors haven't the teeth or the bite for forever. I am beginning to believe they haven't the weight to hold onto a memory. The ground is steadily drying and laying itself out flat before me. The air is cooled and unworried. I sense no treachery awaiting, I sense a confidence approaching.

I have to believe I am the link and the line between where the muses are and where they belong. The ground is transforming into light gardens ahead, they are unfamiliar gardens, but pleasantly so. The jelly between the night and the day has dried. A night I endured for a promise has ended, it was for a promise I would suffer again and again. As I draw closer, I know I have never seen such growth before. There are colors and a thickness, shades and shapes known only to makebelieve. The light gardens gain mass, it all bends awkwardly and almost painfully, in a random frozen dance. There is not an insect to be seen or heard, there is not a single petal on the ground. These gardens appear frozen in a moment of terrible beauty.

I venture further, there are no paths, but there are pauses, there are no trails, but there are hesitations. There is an open slash of bare ground ahead, I can see it as the growth has dropped from my shoulders to my waist. It could be a forgotten place or a mistake or a strike of anger. But I sense it, tingling, just ahead. The curiosity and the whispers of the muses. Calling to me in the only way I can hear, calling to me because Love told them I can be trusted. They   must have taken the path which took me, or they were chased. They must have endured the same night. Whether stolen or forced, carried or seduced, or by purposeful escape, the muses are here. I am waiting to see them, they are waiting to be found. This is not their home, it is the most familiar surroundings they could find, in their flight, in their fright. I am exiting the bulk of the gardens, I am exiting its thickest arms, its thickest sprawl. The air beyond has a solemn, apologetic feel, it is a thin clinging film to walk through. It searches me more than it hinders, it asks questions as it allows me to pass. I sense the muses are gathering, just around the edges, and I do hope they trust me. I can return them to the one who sings to them and dances with them in the water.

The ground is thinning into dirt and choking weeds, it seems to change and wander, in space and size and shape, as though it is trying to find a comfortable way to lay down. The muses are all about, I know, I just know. I pause to allow the comfort of a settling, I pause to allow a calm which they may find familiar. There is going to be an end, and I am thankful, it can be a lightning strike or a slow peel. I don't understand how far we have gone, but I want to be home, and if the muses must ride home on my back or my shoulders or my opened hands, I want to be home, with a kiss for the face I made a promise to in the dark.

And no, no, the ground beneath becomes adrift, it breaks into an island. The last words have not yet been spoken. There are serious and solemn and heavy steps approaching, they carry all that is known, all that has been learned, and all that has been accomplished. The gardens bend further away, this new day stops its plans. There is a sudden hush that seems to be afraid to be here. The hush is afraid to be involved, it is afraid to leave. Everything becomes reluctant, not knowing its place in the line. If the stories are true, this is the awakening, this is the role call, this is the price, and this separates the true from the false.

Now the blind must prove it can't see and the empty must prove it can't feel. The trusted will be tempted and the fearless will run away screaming. Everything will be placed upon its head, and not everything will regain its march, its stance, its importance. This is when the noise weeps and the adventure whimpers. Fire must hold our hands in the cold and the darkness, the past and the future must refuse to dance. There is a harsh line drawn between the takers and the givers.

If the stories are true, when Strength rises from beneath its mountain, when Strength walks with its hounds through its gardens, it wants to take it all back. The hounds sniff about and Strength seeks pleasure. If the stories and whispers and legends are true, it wants all that belonged to it, it wants all that it has ruled, all that it has possessed. It wants the wings and the harmonious things, it wants what was used in slow sleep and slow slumber. It wants to take everything back. Everything borrowed and everything bled, everything gifted and everything stolen. Once Strength is awake and walking, it will feed itself and feed its hounds. All that is misused and unused, all that is purposeless, all that is unneeded and greedy, the hounds are hungry and the hounds are searching, and Strength will feed them.

Strength will tap the two heads of the mountain it lives beneath, and the mountain will walk off with its own legs. Strength will come for what sings, it will come for what has laughter. It will come for what tries to hide from it in dark corners. And I am not spared. I may not be sacrificed, but there is weakness replacing my feet. Strength wants to be called and it wants to be colored, its hounds roam and its arms swing about. It won't be teased or mislead. Strength will taste you and take you, it knows the name your mother and father gave you. It will know you by the spit in your eyes. It will choose whether to return and lift and comfort you, or leave you laying in the messes, the confusion.

I am in its garden and I have no voice and I have no choice. Strength leaves no mysteries, it has no friends or enemies. It has done all for you and you have done nothing in return. It wants its coat back.

My knees soon crumble and I am but a damp place on the ground for it to walk over. I am but a light heave in its garden, I am but a stone upon its path. I look directly at it, I am a face with no questions, I am a borrower and harborer with no crimes. Strength accepts and expands and recedes with no words. That is its way. It roams these gardens for pleasure, it roams and speaks no words, it sees the seeds when it walks with its hounds. It can see your hands and it can see your face and it can watch you grow. My shoulders and elbows join my knees, my mouth is close to the ground and I am trying to speak. To thank it for its gardens, to thank it for its gifts. I know its touches alternately sleep and awaken and I now know its steady heavy stroll. I know its hounds are bound by duty and I know Strength's long forceful walk is reluctant and necessary.

I don't believe I have ever offended it. My face is pressed to the ground, the very ground, this real ground. And Strength walks over me. The hounds have scattered, and this becomes a pool and not a robbery, it is a slow repossession, a slower bath. My hands are empty and my heart is full, and I hope Strength hears it. A vision comes dancing across my eyes and across my lips. I can't see the sun anymore, I can't see this day. But the muses, now that we are alone, they are pressing close around me. They are around my arms and legs, they can't possibly move me. I haven't anything left inside of me to gather them. The muses crawl over me like a wish, they manage to bring my mouth out of the dirt.

Strength has left and I lay still, I have to believe the parade is finished. It has left with a look that wanted to tell me it appreciated the way I carried it and for how long I carried it. I am abandoned but not distraught, I am beyond telling the color of the light from the lights. I can't move to collect the muses, I can't find the words to speak to them. They seem to have forgotten the dances they learned in the roses. They have lost their flight and I fear I have lost everything. I have found them and can not save them. The muses are gathering in numbers and they can not set me free.

A miracle pulls me onto my back. There is a promise upon my lips. There are fingers in the splashes, there is a thud, there is a weight, and I believe this wait will be short. I know I can endure this. There is the absence of Strength and the pale pale taste of surrender. It has no force. My face is off the ground, it is free to see all I can see. It is free to remember all that I have lost. There is the drooping, wilting face of Surrender, surrounded by all I can't hear. It is the emotionless face of Surrender, and everything I haven't the will to refuse to see.

I feel the relentless pull of home, I hear the tone of Love, I taste the tone of Love, I feel the burn and the comfort. I lay still, believing there is more beyond the comfort.

The muses are joining hands and forming long chains, but even with all of them as one, even with their faith and their forgiveness, their impurity, their imperfection, I am an impossible task. I am an impossible burden. Surrender is too cowardly to draw too close. It tries to flip its purpose onto me from a distance. I have breath left only to believe. Surrender is ringing its bells, and whether it is belief or weakness, I can see it, but I can not hear. Surrender is not a journey, it is a flash of a moment. It is an ambush, it finds you only after working in secrecy and stealth. Surrender comes for you, one hair at a time, one bone and one thought and one disappointment at a time. It patiently collects the piles behind you, it is so quiet you don't even feel its shadow.

It will find no satisfaction with me, I haven't been followed, I don't have its footsteps behind me. It hasn't the teeth for me. I haven't been in the marinade, I haven't been lost down its path. And the vultures which follow it, I am not their meal. The day is coming, it might come with warmth or heart, it might come with rain or trickery. It might press me into the dirt. I haven't a shred or a sound or a movement left to resist. But I tell the muses to stay close, because Belief hangs over me, I will see this day's end.

My heart becomes the only sound, it chooses wildness over tenderness, it chooses defiance over calm, it urges the rest of me to will myself, free myself. It urges my soul to choose forever over here and now. It is a battle and a bitter argument I feel the rest of me can not join. My mind is a wordless cloud, my eyes fall to damp slits. The silent sun is upon me. But I have broken this night. Belief is at my lips, with water or poison, and now there is a hand that joins theirs, there are hands I feel about me. I have no more worry and no more will. These hands can drag me or drown me or save me.

Belief's kindness and whispers are trying to kiss my ears. I am so terribly far from what I know. I can't decide if it is too late, I can't decide if there is a next. This time, it is not up to me. There is a hand working its way through the frailty, there is a hand collecting the fragile. There is a hand calling and searching and finding me within the broken pieces. There is a sure and true hand, it points me away from the fall, it points me away from the fail. This hand has a familiar voice within its touch. This hand with lines of centuries wrapping its knuckles and wants of centuries at its tips. A hand tapered and delicate and powerful.

Without feeling my own breath, I know this hand, without opening my eyes, I know this hand. I know the caress I pursued and lost and finally gained. The one I feared I had lost again. This is the only hand that will seek me and reach me through memory and intimacy, through test and trial, through cold and shadow, through agony and calm. This hand holds me without possessing me. It lifts me. It has me. This sweet slender hand that can carry the world, spin the world, change and beautify the world. For all it can do, it pauses to touch my cheek in my moment of excruciating need. I know this hand, I remember every word it has spoken. I know its passion and its determination, I know its warmth and its shelter, I know its comfort.

My lips are brought to an exhausted smile. I feel a lift at my back, I am being raised from the dirt and the ants and the ashes. I am being raised from the terrible weakness I should have never suffered. I know this hand, I longed for it even before I was allowed to pursue it, I longed for it before I feared it had forgotten me. I ached for it and it found me. This hand could do anything, anything at all imagined, and it chose to save me. Again.

When I said 'I do' I remember it feeling and sounding more like I would and always will. There is an 'I know' with fingers upon my cheek. She knows I will always keep my promises.

Love's hand pulls its fingers across my struggles and thanks me for walking into the mess and the sour of a savage night. I would do so a thousand times again, even should I know what awaits. I feel more bliss than weakness, more peace than confusion. This hand is here through the spill, it is here to collect the pieces, all my pieces, and make them whole. Love's hand is upon my brow and at my chest and asking if I am ready to go home. I am not a soldier or an adventurer, I am a dreamer that tastes the redemption of roots. I will never again wander or be lost, until I must. There is a bliss within her hand, there is a leap and a wisdom and a feel found nowhere else in this world.

Love's hand becomes two, I am going to be brought out of the gray and out of the wash, out of this light and back to the truth. I am going home. These hands promise to find me wherever I go. And I promise every inch and sensation within their grip, I promise every year and every mark and every effort they tell stories of, I promise their search and their longing, their fantasy and their function, I promise I am exactly where I want to be.

There is but one more kindness, one more softness, and in one slow gentle motion, a loving pull back into our dance and days.

LEANING

I lean from a dream as Love touches my arm, bringing me a coffee in her other hand. She has watched me as I stood motionless for at least ten minutes. 'Where have you been, Leo?' she says. I have been nowhere and everywhere, I have endured what should not exist. We will not kiss for the silence of last night, we will not kiss for the turmoil of last night. We will not kiss for the loss or kiss for the strain. Love finds me in the morning, she finds me with her magic. She asks, 'Where are you going?'. I am coming home. Somehow, I realize I stood in our place, I stood for us,

I kept the madness from reaching the reason. And Love simmered me as I slept and kept us here, she simmered me and kept me safe.

She has eggs cooking on the stove, and bacon, because she feels I need some relief. She knows because she aches and feels just as I do, she knows because she understands how my legs have stood their ground. I was not reluctant, I was immoveable. It was a night never meant to be ours. From the moment she woke this morning, ever since she can remember, I am this man. The one she loves. I kiss her and thank her for opening the windows and the doors so this day will not smash through them. This is a day that might try to bring the breaking hours, now that the panic of the night is gone. I am tired, so tired, and this day is going to try to linger, it is going to try to keep speaking of yesterday. Love is tired, too, but I will chase every smile she offers with one of my own.

This day is looking forward, it is wearing its long legs, it wants to have a tantrum. I don't wish to speak of last night, it was a lost night, if indeed it was a single night. This day has a fury, and we only feel forgiveness. Place the time and the hours and the steps and the crimes behind us, and let the past handle and suffer the rest. We own a forgiveness, we burn in a forgiveness.

Love has a song at her cheeks, she has a song in her eyes. What is ours is meant to be ours. I sit heavily in a chair, I can feel the dream as though it wasn't. I am in an unmoving comfort, a quiet that won't be quiet. This day is trying to present itself as though it must be endured, it is bringing itself to be dared. I haven't the strength to question, I've barely the strength to rise from my chair.

Love brings me a plate, I touch her hand in a whisper. There is no sickness or suffering here. The pieces are ours. They lay about to be found. Our gardens return, they return with complaints, but they are coming in piles. We were too late for the insult, too late for the fight. But they respect our faith. I watch as the gardens resettle into what they were meant to be. This might be the enchanted, this might be the untold. The sun is dripping gravy, I find Love in her cooling spot. I tell her it looks as though everything is returning to its place, and she smiles beyond my words. We are but a glimpse within the wave, perfect in our own place.

We have nothing which can be stolen. Nothing which can be lost. The Morning has taken her exit. But I am home. The afternoon comes with its heat and its grievances, the afternoon comes as though it wants to bully and bother. But I can see every color the moon has ever known. I can see what can never be forgotten. As a sitting witness in my chair, I feel what was never abandoned or doubted. Even as my legs and my back and my mind could not endure, my heart and my soul, they feel the dance.

The cool of the evening comes, with all the recklessness we know. I have spent the day feeling lost but offering the day a chance to heal. An opportunity to redeem itself. Love shows me all the softness I did not fail. She shows me all the softness I did not lose. I came home with want and need, I came back to us to find nothing had to be sacrificed. All the luscious pleasures and treasures are here. I am back in her wings, back in the tones and hue and truths they weep.

I lean into our moments, into all our hands did not do today. Perhaps it is the universe apologizing. Or the Elements which abandoned us to the chaos have returned, not to right the wrongs, but to erase them. Love reminds me I kept my promise, I kept my word as I always do. This kiss and this harbor all around us is exactly how it should be and must always be. It gives us no urge to bend, no urge to kneel. In the hushed light I am making out the shadows and counting them, I get to 14, 15, 16, and then they reshuffle and I start over again with the new. Some seem demanding and others seem to cast blame. And I feel the shadows are the Elements, and I feel the world is round again.

I struggled last night and now I feel a long coat of forgiveness. There is nothing to share and nothing to burn. There is no defeat and no victory. There are no consequences or rewards. I lean into the lovestains that make their way over the fences. I am easing into the heavy, heavy lovelean. The one that makes us whole, the one that brings us beyond. I am too comfortable to move, too comfortable to be concerned it is becoming dark. We are loveravaged and lovepummeled and everything is right with the world. I do not know where this day went, but Love asks 'Are you hungry?'. And I lean into her like she is a windstorm, I lean into her like she is lightning, like she is salvation.

141

All which can not be broken or stolen, all which the outside eyes can not see and can not find. I lean into the base, into the strength of the pillars, I lean into the fire. I lean into the passion and the fierceness. I lean into the simplicity and the certainty. We are covered in a dust that is lovefrosting. There are lovemeats to eat and lovewines to drink. I lean tighter into the squeeze. Keep us in these barrels and bowls, keep us in this fog. There is love in this tugging dampness, there is love in this suction from this mud. I lean until it appears I am falling. I lean until I am falling faster and deeper.

I lean until our dirty sophistication grabs hold of me, I lean into our dreams that are never forgotten. I lean into the pleasure of the juice. The Elements can hold council tonight, the Elements can wage war if they must. Love and I dare to be two, we dare to be one. We brave the unknown and we brave the mystery and sit willingly and patiently in the heat. I lean into us, I lean into home, and I feel how alive we are. I lean into here and now and I feel their flesh and their teeth. Give me floods tonight and give me peace to lean against.

Love comes outside and I kiss her through the challenges, I kiss her through the soft laughter. The bones in my limbs are the same I carried just a few short years ago. Now they are loveeager and lovelimber. Let's have a little dance. Let me be a lovechild, let me be brave and lovecrazy. I remember the night she showed me the door and showed me how to use it and the tone of her voice when she said it was always free and always open. I remember all the poetry and the distance and the adventure we have discovered, and we have never forgotten our slow easy loveclimb. She can bring me into her arms with the same ease she raises me to the stars, she can bring me to the moon with the same ease as insisting I be at her neck. I am possibly too lovedazzled to be dining at this hour, I am possibly too lovedizzied to be drinking at this hour.

I lean into the sight and scent of Love. 'I know exactly where you are,' she says. I am half in the pudding and half in this world, half in the magic and half in this answer. I can laugh as though I am gripped in the madness, I know why forever grinds its teeth on stones. Because it is delicious. Forever has never been found, it has always been there and never been found. I lean into forever, I know you forever and where you like to hide.

Last night was dreamless and it interrupted the noise, and I leaned into the sweetest captivity. I was inches from heaven. I slept with an angel's hairs across my eyes and an angel's breath in my ears. Laying flat and straight and peaceful had no effect upon the lean. I walk with it and almost want to talk with it, I have some noticeable lovelines on my face, and my hands ache a bit as though they have done some traveling.

I have poured my second cup of coffee before I realize today has no name which stands out. It's another for the pile, another to be thrown upon the pit. It is a log on the fire, it is some sun upon my shoulders. It doesn't need to be washed or dried, it can simply hang in the air. It doesn't stink of nonsense, it doesn't crawl like obligation. It is a gift. It holds no baggage and it has no candles, it has no voice, just an expression asking me what I will do with it.   This is a mighty lean and it makes no difference whether it is heading left or right. I lean forward. I lean within, towards the learned, towards the enchanted. I lean into the secrets she and I share. I put more sugar in the spoon, I don't need the difficult or the bitter, I don't need the tough. There is a gentle stirring, hoping to be released from its corner.

I lean towards kindness, the water wants to be a bath today, pleasure wants to plow today. There is a little strangeness out there I can't count, not even using my fingers. There are some holes to be answered with heat and cold. There are some holes I do not need to see or hear. My eyes are up on my head and my ears are lingering close by. The lean takes me further and further from where the emptiness lays to rest after it plays.

Love comes to me and she has only a little of the nightcandy, a little wet tenderness in her eyes. She marks the hour and I don't want her to leave. I want her to stay for one more touch, one more song. One more laugh. It is dark and I can see our days have left marks in the grass. I have visions of days when our steps marked the sky. I hope she is tightening the chains, I hope Love checks all the locks. I lean deeper into the lovedrag, I lean into its charming swallow, into its tongue and spit. This has been a good day, a day not to be a casualty of the living, this has been a good day to be alive and dressed and undressed, alive and reaching and grasping for answers and finding all the unspoken reasons.

I lean into the lovesweats and the burdens that never come. They blow crossways like silken whips that never tear and hips that talk, their promises sit just at her chin and above her neck. Love places it all upon my cheek, we could unstart it all and fall back to where we are.

It has been decided, who will go and who will stay, who will return and who will wait. Love says 'I am glad your hands were empty today.' I lean into the tremble, I lean into the whispers and the glances. We have no tricks in our memories. There are no stones in our memories. We throw only bodies and gentleness. We gamble and place it all on eternity. The passion holds the meat that leads us down the trail.

And all that sticks and clings in such luscious grips, unspeakable grips. Please give me those lips to struggle with. I lean into the beg and I lean into the found. I live in a palace of moments, in this place built for two and meant for two. I promise I will gently push aside your hair and find the cheeks behind your smiles. I will temper the day and I will temper the night. When there is a flame it will be ours, where there is a touch it will be ours. It may have seemed today was to keep my feet upon this concrete and my shoulders trapped in this doorway, it might seem as though this lean was wasted. I stood as strongly and still, patiently and hopeful, I don't want to be washed clean, I don't want to be straightened out of this lean.

I have two hands in the beauty, ten fingers in the desire, I have two legs for the movement, two feet for the always. We have two chairs. My Love, we both remember, I needed only one chance and we needed only one night. I needed only one taste. I found the nails of hunger and I heard the cries of starvation. Give me one million more reasons. I am so full, and I will find a way.

My Love, let's lean into the stink and the stains, and all their caves and causes and chapters and memories. We can lean into the charms, there is no need to collect them, they will be waiting. Here. And now. My Love, there is the choke and there is the chance we take, there are all the pictures we make and no one else will see. I lean into the moments that are lovesmothered and the juices roll right onto the sharpest points. I lean into this decadence, I love to live with it steaming and dripping. I lean into this certainty, that tomorrow is more beautiful and it will outlast the next.

I lean into the luscious things as they spread themselves across tables and chair and blankets, as they sun themselves and soothe themselves and make themselves feel right at home. They will feed and demolish, they will quietly comfort and conquer. They will have a story and a voice here. They will have a linger and a longing and a bite here. They can explode, they can ask, they can take and give, they can't be controlled and neither can we. We walk along the paths that embrace us, we walk along the paths that whisper as though they created us.

My Love, I am never alone with the luscious things. It would take time for them to be shared or learned. It is best when they seek you in moments of light and moments of truth. I don't pretend to understand everything, I offer myself as a canvas, I choose to have them possess me and speak to me. I would have them clobber and cripple me. I want the luscious things to take the fight from my eyes and the vision from my hands. I want to walk where I don't yet know how to belong. I want the luscious things draped over me, chilling me like icicles, warming me like worrying lava. I want them to invade and think for us and believe for us.

I lean into it all as easy as smoke or fever. I want my fingers in the spaces Love and I occupy. I lean into a blister and a burn, I know who I am and who I have become. The luscious things are all around us, we are their darlings. Here they exist free from the mathematics, free from the sciences, free from the histories. Free from all which might threaten to explain them.

There is a face I know and seek, a face I can not live without. There is a face without trouble, without stress. There is a face with a smile and blue eyes, there is a face that welcomes me home. I lean into a beautiful beautiful face that requires no paint and does not change with the seasons. There is a face I lean to, one I must have. I need no directions to find it.

She keeps the talk from talking, she curls it into lovespeak, never too soft and never too loud. She keeps the walls from walking and crumbling. She keeps the sky high above any misery, she keeps the stars high above any misunderstanding.

Our little gentle world has rediscovered its legs, but there is one sudden change. There is nothing subtle or hidden about the change in the muses. Growth has found them, every last one. And whether it was waiting or wishing which held them here, they are now unkept. The muses are gathered tightly with a purpose and in a silence which can be heard. Love and I can hear it, in the poetry we have come to know. Love and I can hear it, the colors we have come to trust. I am unable to lean into this weight, a new storm is coming and it has nothing to do with us.

Fate is coming, there is no crush or cruelty. Fate is coming with its winds and its songs and its cries. It does not come for Love and I, we were dragged and carried and found and planted long ago. Fate is coming with its long beard and its hands and its purposeful plans. It is coming for the muses, and it paints a path for each one. It is their time. One by one they leave with their eyes and smiles and dances we have become so accustomed to, one by one they leave with their wings and their voices. Whether it is to their destination or simply to a safer place, it is not ours to question. One goes like a rocket, one in a whisper, another like a firefly. One after the next, Fate is taking them closer to home. It guides them and encourages them, it shows them the steps and they are following, it leads them to the edge, and they were born with the knowledge for the rest. There are welcoming and wanting hearts and souls out there tonight.

The last muse vanishes into the journey, and now Fate and its magic leave without a word, just as it arrived. There is nothing to alter here, nothing to teach. There is nothing to pry or prod, there is nothing to save. It has nothing to breathe into and nothing to answer for. Love and I remain here alone in our gardens.

I lean into this new silence, this new fabric which surrounds us. I hold Love's steady hand. We are in paradise, all are welcome, but this paradise has a lean for two.

FINDING

There may be a hint of sadness, but it tastes more like memories, now that the only things to be found beneath the rosebushes are our hands. There are some slight shadows, but I believe they will surely fade and vanish. Nothing has been tarnished, nothing has lost an ounce of beauty. The blooms and colors are proud. Love and I can always be found in the over wash of the luscious things. We are willing to be the prisoners they make us, the prisoners who refuse to escape even when the cages are opened. We are the prisoners and the kept who require no shackles and no guards. We happily share the rule over our little kingdom with all the luscious things. We are prisoners, we are king and queen, with no ask and no position, we are prisoners with no fault and no penance, we are prisoners with a dance.

All we have done is spread the bones, the meat will come as it comes, slow and purposeful, and the rest will be stirred and salted and cured and seasoned. I find they come most every day, to make our home more our home. I find they come and seem to wander and delay, as though they are waiting to be asked not to leave. I find they come as whispering rivers of ideas. The luscious things spread like an evening, or a star shaped flower in the morning, or a kiss, or shade across our shoulders and faces. They are entangled deep within the missing and the held, the willing and the found. I find myself equally appreciative of that which crawls and leaps and that which soars, that which hungers and that which feeds. And all that holds their questions and all that blows their answers upon us.

I find I love her in this moment, more so than the last and perhaps less than the next. No matter what tatters the hours or owns the hours, there are moments. We don't speak of the days we can't remember and the nights we were searching and lost through lives, with voices unheard, hands untouched, kisses unplaced, hearts left unfound. A drip came through a careless pinhole, a pinhole reduced itself to a tear, a tear became a thought, a thought became a promise, a promise became an ache. A true ache. A luscious ache when a soul finds a soul.

Oh, how the luscious things have such an endless curiosity for the depths of our simplicity. Love and I let them drape over us and follow us and listen to our conversations, and then we all laugh together and pretend we do not know. There is the purity of the possession. The living and working, loving and writing, planting and eating and drinking, talking and dreaming and doing. I am slowly finding my way out of my head and back into the light we know. I hope they continue to find us to be their favorite prisoners, now as we drown in their taste. We don't seek pardon or favors or freedom. They lavish us, they speak to us. Our lives and our loves were denied so long but never forgotten and never abandoned.

I find my steps firmly on the edge of what is right and never wrong. Love finds a drink and some relief and we look at each other. She has the lovely look of a woman I have not yet adored enough. There are years that have not been stolen and we don't have to steal. There are years not lent or borrowed, not burned or broken. There is time yet to become. There has been nothing lost. Trust and hope and everything savored are under my sleeves, they are crawling up my arms. They are finding a taste they like.

I find I am no longer on the short side of the mystery and the magic, it lays willing and flat and as long as my appetite. Fifty-seven years does not seem too large of an ask, fifty-seven years before we ask for more. I want to see my Love's eyes in fifty-seven years and see how they burn brighter than they do today. These hands of mine that have had faults may not belong to saints, but there is a beauty that calls me by such sweet names. I am so far from the devastation, I can feel the deliverance. I have been walked beyond the confusion, I have been escorted past the lost. I have been brought into the deep found.

She hums and sings relentlessly through the water and the sunlight, wanting only for our babies to grow. We were all here before the muses, and here we remain. Love and I, and the Elements, and everything we care about.

Love and I haven't spoken of the muses today. It occurs to me, how quickly I speak of them in the past tense. They were not our creations, they were not our possessions. They were a lightness in our lives. They were a pleasure in our lives. I hope the paths the muses took were straight and true, I hope each one has found either safety or their destination. Such is the softness where we live and grow, such is the softness we offer and do not own. I find I do not look into the eyes of the meat before I eat it, I do not look into its eyes before it eats me. I find pleasure has a quiet and chaos has no noise.

We are given this raw day with no expectations. We heal though we have suffered no harm. We stand as we have always been. The light is correcting itself, our gardens resume crawling over themselves. I find the air offers no unneeded apologies, we are dancing as we have always danced. The world's eyes have turned its microscope somewhere else. I find we are inclined to be private, we find the lesser things fill our imaginations. We will take dirt over caviar, and simplicity over luxury.

Love passes with a word and a smile. I believe the voice in the back of my mind can define the taste in the back of my throat. It is swollen satisfaction. Love offers me this steady weightless burn, this scorch with no teeth. I follow just a couple of steps behind her, not because I fear I will lose her, or she will lose me. I simply must be with her. I wonder if I will find the words to fill her world. I wonder if I will find them, out here, today. Love goes inside and returns with what she is. I have found a peace with no price.

When Love returns she says, 'It is Tuesday.' I may have asked and now I know. We can speak idly in the leaves and cherish wildly in the later. I find as this day grows thick and lumbering, our yard has grown heavy and crowded with the Elements spreading as far as my eyes can see. They admire the quiet of the luscious things. I find myself appreciating the hush, either I am not listening to them or they are not speaking today. I find myself with nothing in my hands and nothing in my pockets. It is only Love and I, in our freedom, buried and gifted.

Our little home has felt no tragedy, it has no wounds. We walk with our lives spreading out before us. I find I feel no different today, only that it becomes worse, and I love her more. The outside costs will eventually shake itself into darkness and do us no harm. We can soak ourselves heavy in the soil, we can soak ourselves speechless. We can never be blind or deaf to all the luscious things.

There is an unrelenting certainty, a whisper growing like a hymn the universe knows oh so well and is beginning to sing in a low voice. There is a truth crawling towards us like a chain and each Element is adding a link as it passes. It is coming to find us, and we are waiting. We pause for another word and another kiss. The chain will find us impossible to resist. We are the endless and the richness that stirs this luscious life. The chain will grow and wet our walls and hang like a canopy over us tonight. Because it finds our every charm and memory sweeter than the last.

Every word that has escaped me, my Love, every word I have failed to reach, I will find them. And I will tell you. There is a bite, a feel, a comfort we know and want to share. It is when we leave everything else aside and behind, and say I love you. There is a feel, beyond hands, beyond hearts, there is a feel only souls know. You found me where and when I was waiting. You found me before I was lost.

I read somewhere about living a luscious life, about life having a pleasantly rich flavor and aroma and sense. We are prisoners of it, just prisoners. Here is my chain, here is your chain, here is the kiss that keeps us, here is the embrace that keeps us.

I will find the words that make me yours. Always. Because forever is not enough.

Made in the USA
Monee, IL
17 April 2025

15997796R00085